best buddies

sisters of the heart

soul sister

friends forever

kindred spirits

sister-friends

SISTERCHICKS
Say Ooh La La!

pals for life

girlfriends

chum

gal

true blue

ally

a sisterchick® novel

SISTERCHICKS

Say Ooh La La!

ROBIN JONES GUNN

Multnomah® Publishers *Sisters, Oregon*

SISTERCHICKS SAY OOH LA LA!
published by Multnomah Publishers, Inc.

© 2005 by Robin's Ink, LLC
International Standard Book Number: 1-59052-412-8
Sisterchicks is a trademark of Multnomah Publishers, Inc.

Cover image of women by Bill Cannon Photography, Inc.

Scripture quotations are from:
The Message
© 1993, 1994, 1995, 1996, 2000, 2001, 2002
Used by permission of NavPress Publishing Group
The Holy Bible, New International Version (NIV)
© 1973, 1984 by International Bible Society,
used by permission of Zondervan Publishing House
The Holy Bible, New King James Version (NKJV)
© 1984 by Thomas Nelson, Inc.

Multnomah is a trademark of Multnomah Publishers, Inc.
and is registered in the U.S. Patent and Trademark Office.
The colophon is a trademark of Multnomah Publishers, Inc.

Printed in the United States of America

For information:
MULTNOMAH PUBLISHERS, INC.
601 N. LARCH STREET
SISTERS, OR 97759

Library of Congress Cataloging-in-Publication Data
Gunn, Robin Jones, 1955-
Sisterchicks say ooh la la! : a sisterchick novel / Robin Jones Gunn.
    p. cm.
ISBN 1-59052-412-8
1. Americans—France—Fiction. 2. Female friendship—Fiction. 3. Women travelers—
Fiction. 4. Paris (France)—Fiction. I. Title.
PS3557.U4866S58 2005
813'.54—dc22

                                    2005016983

05 06 07 08 09 10—10 9 8 7 6 5 4 3 2 1 0

To the one and only Anne-girl
who showed me *her* Paris after I vowed I'd never return.
Okay, so you're right, mon ami.
Paris is an amazing city.
And the little cha-cha you danced on the Eiffel Tower
was pretty memorable, too… Sisterchicks forever!

God's Spirit beckons.
There are things to do and places to go!
This resurrection life you received from God is
not a timid, grave-tending life.
It's adventurously expectant, greeting God
with a childlike, "What's next, Papa?"
God's Spirit touches our spirits and confirms
who we really are. We know who he is,
and we know who we are: Father and children.

ROMANS 8:14–16

Prologue

My best friend, Amy, likes to say her first words as a baby were, "Ooh la la!"

She also says her Parisian *grandmere* taught Amy to say *merci* instead of *thank you* and to walk with her shoulders back and her chin forward. From the day I met her, she always has carried herself with a ballerina-like posture. If it's possible for a woman to be elegant at age eight, Amy was.

Amy arrived in our uncouth corner of Memphis in the middle of our third-grade year. She moved into the big brick house on Forrest Avenue with her mother and grandmother. Her mother had flawless creamy skin that made me want to touch her face and hands. Her grandmere spoke only French and wore an expensive perfume that, whenever I got close to her, came home with me in a pillowy after-cloud. At my house, I was the youngest of five and the only girl. Stepping into Amy's pink palace of femininity was my first brush with bliss.

The day Amy entered our class as the new girl, during roll call I studied her long raven tresses. How did she manage to balance her crisp white hair bow so perfectly on the back of her head?

At recess I followed her out to the playground. She turned around and, to my surprise, confided in me as if I were her best friend. "My real name isn't Amy. It's Amelie Jeanette. Most people can't pronounce Amelie Jeanette the right way."

"I bet I can." The advantage of being the youngest with all those brothers was knowing how to accept every challenge and feign fearlessness. That is, until I got hurt. Then I would run away and hide.

Amy raised one of her Elizabeth Taylor eyebrows and waited for me to prove my stuff. I carefully repeated her first and middle names and then added her last name, "DuPree," just to prove I'd been paying attention in class. She was impressed.

I tested her back. "Do you know my name?"

"Of course. It's Lisa Marie Kroeker."

She got my middle name wrong, but I didn't correct her. It was the spring of 1968, and everyone in Memphis, and maybe the rest of the world, had heard the name Lisa Marie that February when Elvis announced he and Priscilla had a baby girl. I liked being called Lisa Marie. Marie was much better than my real middle name, which I had never revealed to anyone.

For an entire week Amy and I were inseparable at school. She brought a package of Hostess Twinkies for lunch every day and always gave me the second one. When I was asked to choose a partner on my day as milk monitor, I chose Amy. It was the happiest stretch of my elementary career and a definite turning point in my no-frills childhood.

My reveling, however, took a nosedive at the end of our first week as best friends when Amy asked, "Do you want to come to my house after school today and play Barbies?"

"Barbies?" I repeated, feeling the walls of our brief Camelot crumble. My mother had unbendable views on Barbie dolls. She said Barbies were "unrealistic" in proportions, "unsavory" as role models, and an "unnecessary" waste of a young girl's leisure time. I rarely was allowed to play with other girls once my mother found out they owned Barbies. Girls who came to my house were expected to play hopscotch.

"I don't have any Barbies," I said.

"That's okay; you can play with mine. I have eight," Amy said. "And two Kens."

My stomach melted. *Eight* Barbies! *Two* Kens!

"Amelie Jeanette." I tried to appeal to something deeper in her than even I understood. "I have to tell you something."

This part of the story is where Amy shines best. She listened, eyes unblinking, as I explained my mother's ban on all things Barbie and her indictment against Ken dolls.

Amy slid her arm around my shoulder. "Leave it to me, Lisa. Your mother will never know."

"But I will," I said, suffering from a strong sense of right and wrong. "I'll know about the Barbies at your house. And the Kens."

"Not if I never take them out of the closet."

"What do you mean?"

With a flip of her ponytail she said, "Whenever you come over, I'll leave them in the closet."

"Amy, are you saying you would give up Barbies for me?"

She nodded.

I blinked almost as fast as a hummingbird's wings and told Amy I had something in my eye. I wasn't used to crying. But then, no other girl had ever been willing to give up Barbies for me.

True to her word, Amy never pulled her Barbies or her Kens out of the closet when I went over to her house. Not even once. I made it through childhood without defying my mother. I saved that delicacy for adulthood.

All Amy asked in return was for a few promises. Some of the promises were sweet, like agreeing to be each other's bridesmaid. Some were silly, like always reading the same Nancy Drew book at the same time and never reading a chapter ahead.

One promise was ridiculous, but I agreed to it anyway. Amy wanted us to go to Paris when we grew up. She said she wanted to stroll down some boulevard called the Champs-Elysées wearing high-heeled shoes and sunglasses. She said that would prove we were stylish. I could use all the style lessons I could get, so I willingly agreed to go with her.

That was before we had a falling out in high school and went our separate ways. We didn't talk to each other for eight years. Such a thing never should have happened to two friends such as we, but that's what happened.

During our separation I formed my own opinions of Amy's beloved France. I came to the conclusion that I never would go to Paris. Not even with Amy. Not even because I promised her I would.

However, I'm beginning to believe that every promise can be heard in the celestial courts, which gives every promise the potential of becoming something of eternal significance. I don't know how it works. I don't know if God really was listening to the "forever friends" promises Amy and I made under the ruffles of her canopy bed when we were young. All I know is that Amy's and my childhood promises were unexpectedly called back into play on a rainy autumn afternoon in the emergency room of Cincinnati General Hospital.

It all started with a not-so-simple "ooh la la!"

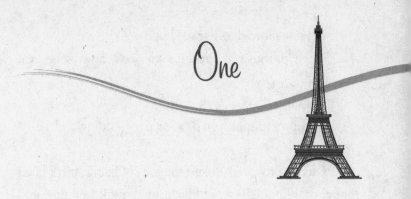

One

The first time Amy made me promise we would go to Paris was on a sultry summer night when we were eleven. A noisy metal fan balanced atop a stack of books on Amy's vanity table provided the only movement in her bedroom. The two of us had positioned ourselves belly-down at the end of her princess bed, chins resting on our folded hands. Facing the fan, we looked at ourselves in all three sides of the vanity mirror. We liked looking in the mirror and making faces at ourselves and at each other. This particular night, however, was too hot to be silly. Amy switched to a different form of entertainment—thinking up things for me to promise her I would do.

"You have to swear something to me, Lisa," she said with her dramatic Amy flair. "You have to swear to me that we will always be best friends, no matter what."

"I'm not allowed to swear," I said.

"Then promise it. Promise me we'll always be best friends."

"I promise."

"And promise me you'll be in my wedding and I'll be in yours."

"Okay, I promise." I liked the idea of being Amy's maid of honor. I knew she would have an all-pink wedding, and there was a good chance I'd wear a very fancy dress.

"Now promise me you'll be there, right beside me, when I give birth to my first child."

"Why on earth would I want to do that?"

"You don't have to watch or help or anything, Lisa. I just want you to be there. Promise me you'll be there." Her expression reflected in the mirror made it clear she wasn't kidding about any of this.

"Okay. I'll be there for you, Amy. I promise."

"Okay, good." Flipping over onto her back, Amy reached for the ruffled eyelet of the canopy with her pointed toe. Earlier that evening we had painted our toes with frosted cotton candy nail polish. I noticed that Amy's toes looked pinker and frostier than mine, so I went for the bottle on the vanity to apply another coat. Keeping up with Amy tended to take extra effort.

"If my first baby is a boy, I'm going to name him Davy," Amy said in her dreamiest voice.

This was no surprise since Amy's closet door was covered with a collection of Monkee fan pictures torn out of her *Tiger Beat* magazines. In the center of the collage was the cover of her mother's *TV Guide* embellished with a red heart around Davy Jones's grinning face.

"Davy is a nice name," I said agreeably. Amy already knew that Peter was my favorite Monkee, so it wouldn't be of any value to bring up that topic again. Ninety percent of the reason I cast my crush vote for Peter was because every other girl at school thought Davy was the cutest. Those were the same girls who had pink vinyl carrying cases for their Barbies.

"Who do you think you and I will end up marrying?" Amy asked.

"Beats me."

"I'm thinking we'll find men who are smart and rich and maybe famous."

I grinned. "I thought you would say they would be French."

"Of course they'll be French!"

Outside, a souped-up car rumbled loudly, leaving behind a puffy gasp of leaded gasoline that rose silently and slipped through the second-story bedroom window to our pristine hideaway. I coughed involuntarily. Anything that had to do with the dirtiness of cars made me cough.

"Unless, of course, I marry Davy Jones," Amy said. "Then maybe we'll just live in France."

I gave Amy one of my "oh, brother!" looks over the top of my glasses.

"It could happen! Of course, you do know, Lisa, that before either of us has babies or gets married, we must go to Paris."

"Why?" I held up my foot in front of the fan in what I'm sure was a rather unladylike pose.

"We have to go to Paris to show we have style. We'll buy high-heeled shoes and sunglasses and parade down the Champs-Elysées like refined and sophisticated women. When we come home, everyone will think you and I are the classiest young ladies in all of Memphis."

Amy seemed to have forgotten that I was the daughter of Tommy Kroeker, as in Tommy Kroeker Deluxe Carwash on Downing Street and Elm. I did not come from a family known for style or sophistication. As a matter of fact, my father was known for his strangely twisted, self-deprecating humor. Instead of minimizing that our last name was pronounced "croaker," he plopped his face on the ten-foot-tall caricature of a bullfrog and turned "Tommy Kroeker's Car Wash" into one of the most memorable sights in Memphis. Before Graceland opened its gates to visitors, that is.

I won't begin to recite all the taunts I heard while growing up. Kermit the frog had not yet made his celebrity debut, and no one yet understood how it isn't easy being green. By the age of six, I was convinced there was nothing positive about being a Kroeker. Especially when you're the only female Kroeker and forbidden to kick or slug or bite, even though you knew you would be pretty good at it if given the chance.

Amy all but dispelled the Kroeker curse that night when she talked about how going to Paris would make me classy and refined. That small seed of hope tucked itself into my spirit and stayed with me for many years before it sprouted.

I look back now and realize that the gift of a true friend is that she sees you not the way you see yourself or the way others see you. A true friend sees who you are inside and who you can become. That's what Amy did for me during those precarious preteen years. She showed me what a beautiful and feminine thing it was to carry around a dream with you. According to Grandmere, Amy said, "Hope is the most versatile and sparkling of all accessories and can be worn by any woman, regardless of her age."

Catching my contorted position in the vanity mirror of Amy's room that evening, I straightened up, and with a heightened sense of my lack of decorum said, "Your mother lived in Paris when she was in high school, didn't she?"

"For two years," Amy said. "Not that you and I have to stay that long. But don't you think my mother is classy?"

No doubt about it. Amy's mom, Elie DuPree, was the classiest of all women. She worked at an exclusive clothing store inside the lobby of the famous Drake Hotel in downtown Memphis. Guests from around the world would ask her advice on what silk scarf matched which leather handbag.

"And what about Grandmere? She's classy, too," Amy continued.

"The classiest," I agreed.

Grandmere used to be a seamstress when she lived in Paris. At only fourteen years of age she sewed clothes for Coco Chanel. Grandmere had an autographed photo of the famous designer framed in silver on her bedroom dresser. I adored Amy's grandmere so much I pretended she was my grandmother, too. Amy knew I was enamored with the three captivating women who filled her house with their lacy laughter. They always welcomed me with a kiss on each cheek and offered me something to eat.

At my house, five boisterous men filled the air with the scent of smelly socks, and after-school treats were unheard of. If Amy came over, and we were absolutely starving, we could eat an apple or a banana before dinner. That is, if my monkey brothers hadn't cleaned out the fruit bowl before Amy and I arrived. My mother, by Amy's confidential assessment, would have made a good pilgrim if she had only been born before the Mayflower sailed.

The crazy thing is that Amy said she liked going to my house as much as I liked going to hers. That was incredible to me. She liked being around my brothers. Amy's father left when she was three. I knew she had long held out the hope that her father would one day step back into her life.

But he never returned. My brothers seemed to fill that loss of male camaraderie in a roundabout way. They taught Amy to play baseball and laughed at what they called her "prissy manners." She loved it whenever one of them chased us with the garden hose.

At Amy's house we sat on velvet-cushioned chairs and learned how to stitch lavender lace sachets for our underwear drawers. At my house we dug up worms for the end of my brothers' fishing hooks. I guess in many ways we both needed each other. While my life provided Amy with roots in the richness of this good earth, she was offering me butterfly wings to soar above it all.

According to Amy, Paris was the nonnegotiable starting point for our flights of fancy. All a young woman like myself needed was to stroll under the Arch of Triumph or saunter past the Eiffel Tower with a well-groomed poodle on the end of a pink leather leash, and I would be transformed into a stunning debutante.

Amy was the one who could make all that happen for me. My part was to simply keep my promise to always be there for her.

"So?" Amy challenged me that night under the ruffled canopy. "Do you promise to go to Paris with me before we have babies and get married?"

"Okay, I'll go to Paris with you. But, Amy, we have to be married first before we can have babies." I lifted my feathery blond hair off my perspiring neck and added with an air of authority, "That's how it works."

"What do you mean? That's how what works?"

"First you get married, and then a baby grows inside you."

"You don't have to be married for that to happen."

"Yes, you do."

Amy tilted her head and looked at me. "Lisa, you don't know how it really happens, do you?"

"How what happens?"

"How a baby gets inside its mother."

"Of course I know."

"Okay, then tell me."

"Well…it…actually, nobody really knows how a baby gets in there. It's a miracle. *The* miracle of life."

Amy let out a low, "Ooh la la."

"What?"

"Come here. Sit next to me, Lisa."

"Why?"

"Because I have something to tell you, and if you don't sit beside me and watch my face the whole time, you're going to think I'm making this up."

With her shoulders back and chin forward, my all-knowing friend revealed to me the specifics of one of life's great mysteries. I believed every word. I had no reason to doubt that Amy would always tell me the truth.

As I look back, I don't think I blamed my mother for avoiding the details that Amy so willingly gave me that night. As a matter of fact, I've always treasured that Amy was the one who told me the truth about where babies come from. Such stunning information is best delivered eye to eye, and that conversational style had never been one of my mother's strong points.

I wondered how Amy knew so much. I remember thinking it might have something to do with the church she, her mother, and Grandmere attended faithfully every Sunday morning. They left the house wearing lace doilies on their heads, carrying strings of wooden beads, and walked the four blocks to St. Augustine's with a peaceful solemnity.

Sometimes our family would drive past them on our way to the largest church in town. My mother would cluck her tongue, and my father would honk the horn and wave at them. I always wondered what kinds of secrets about the mysteries of life they were telling Amy inside that fancy church.

At our church, we got the gospel every Sunday, and it never seemed like extraordinary information to me. Amy said they lit candles at her church. We didn't have mystifying things like that at our church. All we had was a baptismal tub with a drain in the floor behind the choir loft. Sometimes the drain would glug at unexpected times, and my brothers would make rude faces at each other and try not to laugh.

Our family always sat five rows back on the left. Each

of us had our own Bible, and whenever Pastor Mason would step to the pulpit and say, "Open your Bibles with me to…" my brothers would vigorously compete to see who could be the first to find the right page.

One time Will turned the pages so fast he ripped 1 John right down the middle. My father leaned over and swatted him upside the head. I was so embarrassed I started to cry. My mother took me by the hand and led me to the restroom where I received a firm swat on the bottom for "acting up in church."

After that I volunteered to help in the church nursery and discovered that no one thinks you're acting up if you're playing with the babies.

My church experience improved when I reached junior high because we had youth rallies and sports nights at which my brothers always dominated the playing field. Amy came with me all the time and told me how much better my church was than hers because we could play basketball in the parking lot and we had guitar music. Plus all of our songs were in English.

I never visited Amy's church because my parents forbade it. I never understood what they were afraid of. But then, I didn't understand why Amy always ate fish sticks on Fridays, either. My mother was pleased whenever I said Amy was coming to a church activity with me. She didn't know that Amy was coming because we had cuter boys at our church.

Amy's first kiss was behind the closet door in the choir room with one of my brothers' friends. She was thirteen. When she came and found me in the church kitchen, I was helping make popcorn for the youth event going on in the fellowship hall, which is where Amy was supposed to have been, hearing the gospel.

As soon as she told me, I grabbed her by the elbow, took her down the hallway, and said, "You listen to me, Amelie Jeanette DuPree. You are *not* going to get a bad reputation around here. Don't you *ever* go off like that again and kiss any other boy at this church! Do you understand me?"

She was so mad at me she called her mother to come pick her up.

Two days later Amy walked over to my house with a bandanna on her head. She came up to my small bedroom that had pictures of kittens and horses pinned to the wall. We closed the door and whispered so no one would hear us.

"Promise me, Lisa! Promise me you won't let me ruin my reputation," she said tearfully.

"I promise, Amy."

After that, Amy was sparing with her kisses, but she didn't stop her systematic development of a new crush on each of the boys in our class. The longest crush was the one she had on Charlie Neusman. He never responded in kind, and I always thought that bothered her, even though she didn't talk about it.

That's the only explanation I could find for the way Amy acted after Charlie asked me to the prom. He was my first date. The prom was my first dance. It took three days of pleading and discussing before I could persuade my parents to let me go with Charlie.

When I told Amy, she said she was happy for me. The next day she turned strangely quiet. The remaining few weeks of our senior year played themselves out, and she stayed away, always giving me what sounded like reasonable excuses for her disassociation with me and everyone else in my family. I kept waiting for Amy's tempo toward me to change the way the big mood ring she wore on her thumb changed every few hours.

Yet Amy didn't change.

I finally asked if she still had a crush on Charlie or if she wished he had asked her to the prom instead, and she said no. I couldn't think of any other reason she would be mad at me.

At graduation we hugged, and Amy whispered in my ear, "I'm sorry. I'll never forget you, Lisa Marie."

I thought it was a strange thing to say. What was even stranger was the way she couldn't find time to get together and do things the way we did every summer. But we both had summer jobs that kept us busy, and soon Amy and I had drifted apart. She went to college in Kentucky. I stayed home and went to community college in Memphis.

We didn't speak to each other for almost eight years.

Those were fumbling years for me. I went from being the small dot at the end of a long exclamation mark at our house to being a mere speck of a life that could easily be brushed away. I wanted to prove to the world that I was strong. I was woman. I roared! But no one was close enough to hear me.

That is, until Amy rolled back into my life, stretched out on a hospital bed with her abdomen rising under the tight sheet like the dome of a package of Jiffy Pop popcorn.

Two

My meeting up with Amy in the emergency room of a Cincinnati hospital is remarkable since she didn't even live in Cincinnati. I'd only moved there a few months earlier. I was at the hospital that rainy October afternoon because Derrick, a potential new boyfriend, was under observation for slitting his wrist. (Yes, I knew how to pick 'em, back in the day.)

The wrist slitting was an accident. Derrick was at my apartment helping open the box of a new coffeemaker. I handed him my pocketknife, since he didn't have one. He flipped open the blade without watching what he was doing, and the sharp tip caught the wrist on his other hand right on the artery. Blood gushed everywhere.

I wrapped his wrist in a dish towel, told him to press hard, and drove my Honda Civic like a race car to the hospital. Derrick wailed like a puppy. That's when I knew our barely-begun relationship was doomed. My brothers would never let me stay with a man who: 1) didn't carry a Swiss Army Knife at all times, and 2) didn't know how to bleed silently.

Derrick received two stitches in his wrist and a glass of orange juice. A resident psychiatrist came behind the drawn curtain and asked Derrick if he had been depressed lately. Catching on to the assumption being made, I explained that the wrist slitting was an accident.

Derrick, however, reviewed a variety of recent maladies for the psychiatrist, including a sore elbow, a ringing in his right ear, a popping sound in his ankle, and occasional swollen eyelids, which he thought might be the onset of lupus or mononucleosis. He couldn't decide which one.

The straight-faced doctor ordered a round of tests, which surprised me. It must have been a slow day in the emergency ward. A nurse suggested I wait in the lobby. That's when I saw Amy. Or, I should say, that's when I *heard* Amy.

A hospital assistant was rolling a very pregnant dark-haired woman in a wheelchair past me and into the curtained area across from Derrick. The attendant helped her up onto the hospital bed, and she let out a long *oooh-oooh*-sounding groan.

I paused and turned to look at her again. When most people moan or groan, they use sounds such as *owwww* or *ohhhh.* Amy was the only person I'd ever heard groan as if she were slowly saying, "ooh la la."

Waiting until the sheet was pulled taut over the woman's middle and the head of the bed was elevated, I got a good look at the patient. My heart pounded.

"Amy?" I stepped closer to her bed.

She halfway opened her unmistakable brown eyes and squinted at me.

"Amy, it's Lisa."

"Lisa?" She tried to sit up and reach out her hand to me just as another contraction overtook her. "Lisa!"

I dashed to Amy's side and grabbed her hand. She squeezed with a force I'd never felt in all our years of Red Rover, Red Rover.

"Don't leave!" Amy cried breathlessly. "Don't let go, Lisa."

I promised her I wouldn't leave; I wouldn't let go. And I didn't.

In between contractions Amy gave me one of her biggest, bravest smiles. "I can't believe you're here!"

"I can't believe *you're* here," I said. "What are you doing in Cincinnati? Last I heard you lived in Lexington."

"We do. Mark's brother is getting married tomorrow. We drove up for the wedding. Mark is at the airport picking up his parents."

"And Mark is…" I was fishing for the answer I hoped would be evidence that she had followed the "first comes love, then comes marriage, then comes baby in the baby carriage" principle for her life.

"Mark is my husband."

I smiled and adjusted her pillows.

"He's a college professor, Lisa. Can you believe I married my college professor? We were almost a campus scandal."

Somehow I knew that made the romance even more delicious in Amy's mind. I looked forward to hearing all the details. At the moment another contraction was coming over her tense frame. With another "ooh," a minute later she released her grip on my hand. Her eyes were still closed and her speech slow as she said, "Mark is shuttling relatives. All day. To the hotel. He doesn't know I'm here."

I stayed with Amy for the next contraction and then left long enough to try to place a call to their hotel and contact Mark. Since this was in the days before cell phones, I had no success in reaching him.

Four and a half hours later, Jeanette Marie Rafferty came into the world. She was five weeks before the due date but weighed seven pounds one ounce and had a full head of black hair. Nothing "preemie" looking about Jeanette!

Mark arrived breathless after Jeanette was rolled up in a pink blanket. The poor guy could barely speak. He had no idea Jeanette Marie had entered the world until after she squealed her first "voilá!" I watched the gentle giant of a man take the infant in his arms and look adoringly at his wife as tears puddled in his eyes.

Slipping out of the room to give them a moment in private, I, too, teared up. Clearly Amy had married a good man. Mark was nothing like my brothers, and for that I was thankful. I did notice, however, that he was not French.

And neither was Derrick.

I found Derrick watching TV and sipping 7UP from a straw. All the tests had come back clear. The doctor told Derrick he was going to be just fine. He slipped into the car holding his wrapped wrist and waited for me to close the door for him. That's when I gave him my diagnosis for our relationship, which was not just fine. No surprise. Check another potential boyfriend off the list.

Over the weekend I visited Amy twice in her hospital room, each time armed with an outrageously large gift basket brimming with the cutest baby girl items I could find and a few treats for Amy. She was sleeping each time so I tiptoed out with my basket, wondering if I'd see her before they drove home.

On Monday she was discharged from the hospital, and Mark insisted they stay at the hotel a few more days before driving home. I took the afternoon off of work and arrived at the hotel, toting my oversized gift basket and feeling strangely shy.

Did I overdo the presents? Would a simple boxed sleeper

set have been a better way to go? Maybe I should have bought Amy a single bottle of lotion instead of the six-piece home spa set.

Too late to change my mind. Mark opened the hotel room door with his daughter cradled in his free arm. Amy called to me from the bed, "Lisa, you came!"

I gave her the audaciously brimming basket of gifts and confessed to my clandestine hospital visits. Amy gave me a scolding for not waking her on my visits, but her hands already had untied the bow, and she was pulling out all the fun gifts.

Her favorite was a stuffed giraffe with a polka-dotted bow around its neck. She practically squealed when she found the extravagant spa set of lotion and bath oils for her. In a way I felt as if I'd finally made up for the birthday when her only gift from me had been a Bible.

My mother was the one who insisted I give Amy a Bible for her twelfth birthday, which Amy graciously thanked me for when she opened it. All the other girls at the party gave Amy gifts like Bonne Bell frosted lip gloss and Jean Naté cologne.

I was so embarrassed that I announced in front of everyone I had another present for Amy at home, but I'd forgotten to bring it. The guilt of my lie made me sick to my stomach. I couldn't keep down the piece of strawberry cake and Neapolitan ice cream, which I urped up in the bathroom. I left Amy's party in quiet humiliation.

The next day I confessed my lie to Amy, and she said, "I know."

"Aren't you mad?"

"No, why would I be mad?"

"Because I just told you. I lied. I don't have another present for you. All I gave you was a Bible."

"I know. I always wanted my own Bible. It's even more special because it came from you. Everyone else gave me stuff I'm going to use up. You gave me something I'm going to keep for the rest of my life."

I was absolved that day and immediately stopped punishing myself.

Standing by Amy's hotel bed now, watching her delight in all the gifts for her and Jeanette, made me feel absolved once again.

Jeanette began to squirm in her daddy's arms. I couldn't take my eyes off the beautiful infant.

"May I hold her?" I asked eagerly.

Mark handed off his precious cargo and reached for the list of baby supplies Amy had prepared for him. "You sure you'll be okay if I go to the store?"

"Of course!" She looked up at me with a bright smile. "We're going to be fine."

I took Amy's words to heart, as if she were uttering a blessing for the next season of our friendship. We were going to be fine. I just knew it. I also dearly hoped that, after all my moves and job changes, things were about to be fine for me in every way. If nothing else, I'd have Amy to stand beside me while I tried to put together the pieces of my erratic life. That possibility brought me great comfort.

Mark slipped out the door as I rocked the baby back and forth.

"Lisa, I love all these gifts." Amy arranged them on the bed for further viewing. "I haven't even had a baby shower yet! It's supposed to be this Friday. Won't they be surprised when I show up with a baby! These are the first presents anyone has given us. Thank you so much."

"You're welcome. I was worried that maybe I overdid it."

"Are you kidding? Overdoing it with gifts? Never! Look how cute this is!" She held up a bib that was trimmed with yellow ducklings. "Thank you again. Really. Thank you for being at the hospital on Friday and for coming today."

"I honestly didn't have much to do with the hospital encounter."

"I know." Amy put down the bib and looked at me with her huge eyes. "God did that, didn't He? Just for us. You promised to be there for me when my first baby was born, remember? I think God heard that promise. There's no other explanation."

I didn't have another explanation so I nodded and agreed with Amy that something mysterious and larger than us was at work. It had been several years since I'd been to church, so I didn't think God was paying much attention to me. I certainly hadn't been paying much attention to Him. I wanted to wait until I knew He would be proud of me before I showed Him the report card of my life. Sadly, a few too many semesters had passed, and I still didn't feel as if I had done anything worthy of His watchful eye.

"Come sit down." Amy patted the side of her bed. "Would you think I was crazy if I said I've dreamed about this? About you and me connecting one day when we least expected it? I've missed you, Lisa. I've thought of you a million times over the years. When Mark and I got engaged, I tried to find you, but I didn't know your parents had moved from Memphis. I sent a wedding invitation to an address I got from your brother Will in Indiana, but it came back with no forwarding address."

"I know. My family is scattered. My mom and dad moved to Florida. Two of my brothers are in Texas. Will is in Ohio now, and Tom moved to Alaska."

"Wow. I can't believe your family is so dispersed. You're here alone then? In Cincinnati?"

I nodded. "I've only been here for three months. Before that it was Houston for a year. I've moved a lot. There's not much to tell. No exciting news. No interesting men in my life. Which is okay; I'm used to living with my own schedule."

I thought for sure Amy would read into my answer that I was still trying to figure out who I was and what my life was supposed to be about. I waited for her eyes to narrow in a judgmental expression. A woman my age should have those basics under control by now.

Nothing but openness and acceptance beamed from Amy's flushed face. She loved me. Still. After all these years. She loved me with the same childhood innocence and acceptance I'd first experienced when she gave up Barbies for me. I choked up because, in the haphazardness of my life, I realized Amy might be the only person on this planet who truly loved me just as I was.

"I've missed you, Amy," I heard myself say as my throat tightened. "I've missed you more than you can even imagine. I hate that I let a date to the prom come between us. Especially a date with Charlie Neusman, of all people."

Amy tilted her head and gave me a look of nonrecollection. "Lisa, Charlie Neusman had nothing to do with our friendship freezing up."

"He didn't? But the prom and—"

"Lisa, I pulled back because of your mom."

"My mom?"

"Yes, your mom and the salvation paper."

"The what?"

Amy's jaw lowered. "You didn't know about that?"

I shook my head. Baby Jeanette stirred in my arms.

"Oh, Lisa, I should have realized you didn't know. I was so blind. I'm so, so sorry." Tears rolled down her cheeks.

"I don't understand. What salvation paper are you talking about? What did my mother say to you?" I instinctively drew tiny Jeanette closer.

With a steady breath, Amy unfurled a story of how my didactic mother had written out a page of Bible verses that related to salvation. When I wasn't in the room, my mother laid the paper in front of Amy, asked her to read the verses aloud, and then asked Amy if she wanted to be saved. If the answer was yes, a line was provided at the bottom of the page for Amy to sign and date.

I felt sick. I didn't know what to say.

"I didn't sign the paper, and that really upset your mom. I guess I didn't know exactly what it meant. I assumed that unless I signed it, I no longer was welcome to hang out with the Kroeker clan. That's why I pulled back from you. I thought all of you felt the same way."

"No. No!" I couldn't stop shaking my head. "Amy, no."

She dabbed her tears with the edge of the bedsheet. "Lisa, I should have talked to you about this right away. I can't believe I didn't. I told my mom what happened, and she said that since all your brothers had moved out by then and you were the only one living at home, I shouldn't do anything that might alienate you from your mom."

"But Amy, I've always felt alienated from my mom. I still am."

"Oh, Lisa, I am so sorry." Amy reached over and grabbed my wrist. "We have to start over, you and me. This is our fresh start. From now on you and I have to be there for each other, no matter what. No more isolating ourselves for any reason! No prom dates or mothers or…or…typhoons can come between us."

She gave my wrist a firm squeeze. "Promise me, Lisa. Promise me we'll start over. I've never found another friend like you. We're sisters, you and I. We never should have been apart the way we were. We have to stay in each other's lives from here on out. Promise me."

"I promise."

For the next forty minutes, baby Jeanette slept in my arms while Amy and I opened our hearts to each other. Amy's bed always had been such a lovely place for telling secrets and making vows. That day, on her hotel bed, was no different.

Amy eagerly told me about how she had met Mark when, as a college student, she went to a campus Bible study. He was the faculty sponsor.

"If you can believe this, your mother's salvation paper actually started my first conversation with Mark."

I winced, but Amy laughed. "No, it was a good thing. I kept that paper in the back of the Bible you gave me. The second time I visited the Bible study, I pulled out the paper and asked Mark questions about each verse your mom had listed. Mark patiently explained how Christ had made a way for me to come to God. I saw it all in the verses. I was being offered the chance to receive forgiveness and to enter into a new life, eternal life, through Christ. I hadn't understood that before. A light went on for me, and I believed. I received." She was beaming.

I sat very quiet, listening. How strange to know that now I was the one hiding in the shadows while Amy was the one walking boldly in full light. Growing up I'd been told our family and our church possessed all the truth while Amy, her mom, and her grandmère were in the dark. We were told to pray for them. I dearly wanted Amy, who was now so full of life that she was brimming over with babies, to pray for me.

"So, see, Lisa? Everything your mom was trying in her own way to give me came to me at the right time. As a gift. From Christ. I know now that's what your mom wanted all along. Salvation. In the end, her less-than-tactful approach didn't hurt me at all."

"But it hurt us," I said.

"Yes, for a little while. But look! We're back together now. At just the right time."

Amy smiled softly, and I felt my curled-up spirit unfurl for the first time in ever so long. I took a deep breath.

"Mark says there are no maverick molecules in the universe. Everything works together according to God's design. I don't hold anything against your mother, Lisa. I really don't. I hope you don't, either."

In that moment I didn't. I couldn't. All I could do was receive. In the same way that I tenderly held tiny Jeanette in my arms, I realized God had been holding me as a baby believer for many years. It was time to grow up. This time in my spirit. And once again the journey would be along-side the one and only Amelie Jeanette DuPree Rafferty.

Oui!

Three

I mark that afternoon in the hotel room with Amy as the beginning of my adult faith journey. So much changed that day. I tossed out my list of potential boyfriends along with my list of dead-end jobs. With only a little coaxing from Amy and a little more coaching from Mark, I moved to Lexington and slowly finished my college degree. By the time I had my teaching credential, little Jeanette was seven and had a five-year-old sister, Elizabeth, and a two-year-old brother, David. I smiled at the memory of Amy's favorite Monkee every time I heard her call her son Davy.

My first decade in Lexington didn't produce any spikes in my static love life. I was busy and happy, though, and involved in a solid church community. Lots of love came my way as an honorary member of Mark and Amy's extended family. I found it ironic that Amy was now the one with a large family and I was "Aunt Lisa," who lived in a nearby condo with pretty frills and an expansive collection of videos, which seemed to be the equivalent for Amy's children to having an enviable collection of Barbies.

My mission, I decided, was to slip Amy's kids Hostess Ding Dongs and Sno Balls every chance I could. Amy's objective was to make her kids do their chores, eat their vegetables, and write thank-you notes for every gift they received. She also insisted that her girls learn to hit a baseball and sit up straight in church.

We were becoming each other's mothers! Only better versions. At least in our opinions.

Amy and I had established a settled rhythm to our friendship. We both acted as if we knew everything about the other. Then one summer afternoon I shocked Amy without meaning to. And then she shocked me right back.

We were making the rounds to the neighborhood garage sales when we came across a metal fan like the one that kept us cool in Amy's bedroom when we were growing up.

"Look at this price tag!" Amy said. "Fifty dollars for what they're calling a 'vintage' fan. Vintage! How do you like that? You and I aren't old enough to be vintage."

"No, but your mother's old fan was vintage. Doesn't it make you feel nostalgic?" I touched the base of the solid fan. "I should buy it just so we can turn off the air conditioning one night and lie on our stomachs in front of the clanking fan and reminisce."

Amy smiled. "Remember the night we promised to be in each other's weddings?"

"How could I forget? That was the night you told me where babies come from."

"That's right. Wow, it seems so long ago. If I never thanked you yet, Lisa, thanks for being there for me when each of my babies was born. And thanks, too, for all the other promises to me that you've kept."

My conscience felt a nudge. I'd been meaning to tell Amy something for a long time, but the right opportunity never came up. Drawing in a deep breath, I plugged the nose of my subconscious and plunged into the deep end of a topic I knew could potentially drown me.

"Amy, I have to tell you something. I didn't keep one promise."

"What? The bridesmaid promise?"

"No, the promise I made about going to Paris with you."

She put down the green vase she had been examining on the "Everything Fifty Cents" table. "What are you talking about?"

"I went to Paris. Without you."

Amy laughed. "Right! You went to Paris, Kentucky, for lunch last month on my birthday. So did I. Remember? I was the one the waiters sang to after they brought over the chocolate cake."

Amy's favorite restaurant was located next to an

antique store in the Lexington suburb. She loved to drive out of town, past the world-class thoroughbred pastures, and visit the darling lineup of shops in Paris, Kentucky. She always came home with a box of pastries from the Bon Jour Bakery.

"No, Amy," I said firmly. "I went to the real Paris. In France."

"When?"

"The summer I was twenty-two. I went with some women from work. We traveled to Paris and London."

Amy looked at me closely. "You're not making this up. You really went to Paris."

I nodded.

"Why didn't you tell me before?"

"Because, well…because I knew I'd feel awkward— which is exactly how I feel right now. I knew how much going to Paris meant to you. I didn't want you to…"

"To what? Be mad?"

"Yes. And I didn't want to feel as if I betrayed you or something."

Amy took slow steps across the driveway and headed for where I'd parked the car under a shady elm tree across the street. Instead of getting inside, we stood next to the car while Amy thought. I knew it was best not to say anything, even though I had so much to say, now that the subject had finally been brought out into the open.

After a few moments, Amy drew back her shoulders. "How was it? Paris, I mean."

"It was terrible."

"No, really. Tell me."

I leaned against the trunk of the supportive tree. "I didn't like Paris at all."

"You didn't? You really, truly didn't like Paris?"

"No. Amy, Paris is not what you think. It's a big city, and I think it's awful."

Amy looked perplexed all over again. "How could Paris be awful? It's the most romantic city in the world. The City of Lights. Everyone loves Paris."

"I didn't."

Now Amy was the one studying my expression.

"Seriously, Amy. I don't want to go back to Paris again. Ever."

I hated bursting her pink, puffy, poodle-bubble. This uneasy moment was exactly why I'd avoided the conversation all these years.

Before I could think of something to say that would smooth over my assessment of Paris, Amy lifted her chin, looked me in the eye, and with one defined eyebrow raised she asked, "What was his name?"

The hair on the back of my neck stood up. "Whose name?" I tried to keep my voice steady.

"The name of the man who broke your heart in Paris."

At that moment I loved Amy for knowing. I wanted to

throw my arms around her and finally release all the hurt and sorrow I'd carried with me ever since the day I was left standing alone at the Gare du Nord train station.

I was just about to tell Amy everything when a horrible screeching sound came toward us followed by a world-rocking wallop of a thud. We jumped back as a red truck turned my already ailing Honda into an accordion.

Amy and I didn't get to finish our conversation for years. Because the crash diverted us into another topic: marriage. That day I met my husband.

Trevor, the driver of the car, missed his family's driveway and hit my car while fiddling with the radio knob. Ronnie, my soon-to-be husband's youngest son, was in the garage at the time and came running out to the elm tree. The entire neighborhood, it seemed, came out to peer at the shocking accident scene. The boys' father, Joel, appeared and calmly made sense of the chaos. His wife had passed away when the boys were young, and Joel was accustomed to "managing the mess," as he called it.

Our first "date" was to the insurance claim adjustor's office. Our second "date" was to the used car lot five days later. By the third date (this one actually included food—Milky Way candy bars from the snack machine at the credit union where I signed papers for the loan on my new Jeep Wrangler), we both knew we were going to keep meeting like this for the rest of our lives.

Joel and I were married when I was thirty-seven and

he was forty-two. To Amy's delight, Joel had a pinch of French blood in him on his dad's side. I moved into Joel's house with the sheltering elm tree where our smashing first encounter took place. Fitting into the lives of three men came easily for me. Within a few short years, both the boys were out on their own, and Joel and I were as settled in as if we had been married for thirty years instead of only half a dozen.

That's when the subject of Paris presented itself again.

This time it was Grandmere's doing. The dear woman had passed away several years earlier, and Amy's mom decided she was ready to leave the brick house on Forrest Avenue and move to Paris. Paris, Kentucky, that is.

Amy coerced me into going with her to Memphis to pack up her mom's belongings. We planned to make the move from Tennessee to Kentucky over Memorial Day weekend sans husbands, since both of them had been planning a camping trip complete with pup tents and fishing poles. Neither of them expressed too much disappointment when Amy and I announced we wouldn't be joining them. Amy's girls quickly made plans with friends for the long weekend, and we all went our separate ways.

Armed with as many collapsed packing boxes as we could rustle up, Amy and I took turns at the wheel of a rumbling U-Rent truck for the eight-hour drive to Memphis. We packed boxes with fervor, swallowing a tear each time we wrapped one of Grandmere's flower-painted glass dessert plates or sorted towels that had been embellished with her handiwork decades earlier.

When we reached Amy's old room, the nostalgia engulfed both of us. Very little had changed in that pink room. The faded, sagging canopy over the bed came down with sneeze-inducing dust clouds and went in a Dumpster. We found my long-missing navy blue sweater under the bed along with an unopened roll of Necco candies that by all appearances seemed as fresh as they were thirty-plus years ago.

On the top shelf of Amy's closet we discovered a black vinyl Barbie case, with one blond Barbie and one Ken tucked inside.

"Why, hello there, Barbie," I said in a deep voice, taking the Ken doll and walking him toward the Barbie in Amy's hand. "Would you like to go to the dance with me?"

"Why, Ken!" Amy answered in a squirrelly voice. "I never thought you'd ask!"

We walked the dolls across the top of Amy's bed. Then, because the only dance they could do with those stiff arms was "The Monkey," we knelt beside the bed, and I defied my eighty-four-year-old mother by playing dancing Barbies. And I was the one playing with the Ken, no less! I felt a strangely smug sense of "so there!"

"You know what?" Amy pulled her Barbie off the dance floor, ruining all my fun. "Your mom was right."

"Don't say that."

"Well, she was. Look at this doll. The body proportions are unrealistic. I mean, look at these legs. Barbie has no thighs. How many real women do you know have no thighs? And this waist. Yeah, right!"

"Come on, Barbie," I said in my best Ken voice. "The night is still young. Let's dance some more."

"I'm going to the refreshment table, Ken," Amy said in her Barbie voice. "I've decided it's time I got myself some thighs. And maybe a little jelly roll around my middle, too."

"I'll join you. What's for dessert?"

"Oh, Ken, you're so supportive! After all those years of being locked up in that box, and yet just like me, the first thing you think of when you get out is chocolate!"

We laughed impishly, and Amy added in her Barbie voice, "You know what *stressed* is spelled backward, don't you, Ken?"

I couldn't switch the letters fast enough to figure out the answer, so in my Ken voice I said, "Ahh, it starts with a *d*, right?"

"Why, yes, it does, Ken. You're so smart! The answer is *desserts*. Get it? Stressed? Desserts?"

I cracked up and said in my own voice, "How did you ever figure that one out, Amy?"

"I heard it somewhere."

We laughed and switched back and forth from our

Barbie and Ken voices as we finished clearing out the remains of the closet and stacked the boxes in the living room.

The last room to pack up was Grandmere's bedroom. I think all of us kept that one till last because every time we went in there and opened the closet, we caught a faint wisp of her perfume or spotted an article of clothing we remembered her wearing. Grandmere had been gone for more than four years, and yet everything remained in neat order, as if she might return any day now from her long journey.

"The new owner wants to keep the bed," Amy's mom said. "But I told them I was taking the bedding."

Amy and I pulled off the comforter and the sheets. I lifted the top mattress so Amy could gather the dust ruffle and there, under the mattress, was a satin envelope purse that was padded like a small pillow. Grandmere's embroidered initials appeared in the lower right-hand corner.

"*Qu'est-ce que c'est?*" Amy asked, switching to French and looking at her mother.

"I don't know what it is. It looks as if Grandmere made it."

I dropped the mattress, and the three of us sat on the edge of the bed, lined up like three twittering birds on the edge of a fence rail.

"Go ahead. Open it." Mrs. DuPree said.

Amy unlooped the elaborate closure, placed her hand inside, and pulled out a handful of crumpled bills. She also pulled out an ivory linen note card sealed with wax and embossed with Grandmere's initials.

"It's for you," her mother said. "It has your name on the envelope, Amelie."

We all glanced at each other as if we had found buried treasure. *What if we hadn't lifted the mattress to remove the dust ruffle?* I thought. *The new owners of the bed and this house would have been in for quite a surprise one day when they moved the bed.*

Amy broke the wax seal, opened the envelope, and blinked at the handwritten note. "It's written in French, Mom. I'm going to need some help."

Between the two of them the message was translated and the meaning made clear. Grandmere had saved all the money she had received for her seamstress work since they had moved to Memphis. Every dollar had been tucked into the elegant satin purse so Amy could use the collected sum to "experience the one thing I have longed for but will not do again in my lifetime."

"What did she mean?" I asked.

"Paris!" Amy and her mom said in unison.

"She always wanted Amelie to go to Paris," Elie DuPree said with a wistfulness I found as intoxicating as I had when I was a child. She always pronounced Paris as the French would, *Pair-ee*. And *Pair-ee* rhymed so nicely with *Amelie*, as in "Amelie must go to Pair-ee!"

The only answer that rhymes with "Amelie must go to

Pair-ee" is, "*Oui, oui, mon ami!*" And that, I knew, meant, "Yes, yes, my friend."

The question was, had I moved far enough away from my disastrous experience in Paris to answer Amy with, "Oui, oui, mon ami"? Then I realized a bigger question was whether I was still on Amy's potential guest list.

"Look, Mom." Amy turned over the note. "There's more on the back."

Elie translated for both of us. "Return to the linen shop of the du Bois family on Rue Cler and bless the family that first put a needle and thread into my young hands."

Amy looked at me, her eyes sparkling. "How much money do you think is here?" She emptied it all in her lap.

She and I sorted and piled the cash with the same excitement we had shared the summer we set up our lemonade stand on the corner and hocked our overly sweetened wares for a dime a cup. Our take that day had been $4.10—enough to get us both into the air-conditioned roller skating rink for an entire afternoon. We practiced our spins in the center of the floor until our knees were bloodied and our egos bruised.

After that we both thought we would do better at tap dancing. Yet we never were motivated enough to earn the amount needed for even one lesson.

From Grandmere's purse we extracted a total of $9,352.

"Ooh la la," Elie said under her breath.

Amy didn't say anything. She left the stacks of money on the bed as the three of us went back to work, side by side, silently packing up the remaining earthly treasures of a woman who had lived with seamless poise and left a silent gift behind for her only granddaughter.

I kept thinking about how $9,352 represented an awful lot of tiny stitches. And all of those stitches had been made after Grandmere was fifty years old.

Not until we had sorted, organized, and packed up Grandmere's belongings did Amy say anything. "I have a question for you, Mom."

As I hung back, Amy asked her mother if she would go to Paris with her.

The DuPree graciousness shone through as Amy's seventy-eight-year-old mother said, "Amelie, you will enjoy your first trip more if you aren't waiting for me to catch up with every step. I have my memories. It's time for you to gather your own. Promise me you'll go while you're young."

Amy and I were forty-four, and that didn't feel young to either of us. We had a hard time figuring out how we had grown that old so fast. But then, I'm sure Amy's mom would have said the same thing, if we asked her.

I thought Amy would invite me on the Parisian adventure next, but she didn't. We slept in a forest of boxes that night and the following. In between sleeps, we worked hard to designate every box either for Elie's new place at

Monarch Manor or for "storage," which was Mark and Amy's garage.

Amy didn't bring up the Paris trip again until Monday afternoon when the three of us were seated in the front cab of the U-Rent truck heading for Kentucky. We were following the moving van that contained all of the furniture and dozens of the boxes. The experience of sifting a lifetime of belongings down to the essentials that would fit into a two-room living space had been sobering for all three of us. No one thinks she is materialistic until she has to decide what to give up and what to keep.

For the past few days I'd watched Amy's mom tell her stories about lamps and porcelain curios simply because we were there to listen. That had been my gift to this woman who had filled my childhood with all the sweetness and frills that had never sprouted in the garden my mother had planted for her children. The DuPree women planted daffodils and forget-me-nots in the garden of life. My mother raised eggplants and parsley.

When traffic on I-40 slowed down, Amy released a telling sigh. I knew that sigh. She was resolved.

"Lisa?"

"Yes?"

"I've been thinking."

I had been thinking, too, and was pretty sure I knew what she was going to say. She wouldn't ask Mark to go to Paris with her. Mark was a lot like my husband. Both Mark and Joel were great at family road trips to Lake Michigan or mission trips with the youth group to any place the old church van would take them. Mark enjoyed fishing for hours from a collapsible chair set up on a river's edge.

Asking a man like that to fly across the Atlantic for the first time in his life to look at statues and buildings and art, to take pictures under the Eiffel Tower, and then to top it off by sipping dark coffee at a cramped sidewalk café where no one was speaking English was more than Amy would be willing to ask of her husband. He would be lost and silent the entire time and ruin the ambience for her. We all knew that.

Amy's daughters weren't ready for Paris. Bright Jeanette was immersed in her job at a local pizza place that doubled as the meeting spot for all her friends. Her college plans were in full swing. Amy's thirteen-year-old, Elizabeth, was a lot like her father when it came to vacation preferences. Lizzie forever had a paperback novel in her hand and would undoubtedly rather read about Paris than actually go there.

In the end, I was the best choice for Amy's travel companion to Paris. She had asked me to go with her three decades ago. I was pretty sure she was going to ask me again.

"Lisa, I want to ask you something, but you don't have to give me your answer right away."

"Okay."

"I want you to think about going to Paris with me."

"Of course I'll go to Paris with you." I grinned. "I told you I'd go all the way to Monarch Manor and help you unload this stuff at your mom's new place."

For a moment Amy didn't catch my silly joke. Then she looked irritated. "No! Not Paris, Kentucky. I mean the other Paris."

"The one with the big pointed tower and the fancy cathedral where the hunchback lived?"

Ignoring my poor attempt at humor, she pushed through the conversation. "Lisa, I know you said a long time ago that you would never go to Paris again, but I'm asking you to reconsider. That's all. Just reconsider."

Amy's mom reached over from the passenger's seat by the window and patted both of us on the leg. "I think this is what Grandmere hoped for all along."

"Amelie Jeanette," I said, "I would love to go to Paris with you. I'm honored that you asked. My answer is oui, oui, mon ami!"

"*Très bien!*" Elie clapped her hands.

Amy added a trainful of celebratory French words, and we began to make plans. I'd become so adept at packing up the past at Amy's childhood home that I subconsciously covered my previous memories of Paris with a layer of invisible bubble wrap. Then I taped the heart bundle so tightly closed that no one, not even my dear hubby, knew a wound hid under the padded layers.

Four

As soon as we decided on our target date for going to Paris, Amy set about with determination to lose weight. Our departure date was April 14 of next year, so that gave Amy eleven months. She stocked her kitchen with tangible assistance from the health food store: protein powder; soy supplements; and a large, dark bottle of Norwegian fish oil capsules.

I watched her one morning as she drank a quarter cup of raw unsweetened cranberry juice followed by half of a fresh lemon squeezed into a cup of warm water.

"Are you sure that's good for you?" I asked.

"It's supposed to revitalize my liver." She then methodically partook of a tablespoon of finely ground psyllium husks to clear the "preservative residue" from her colon. She had been reading a variety of books on nutrition and reminded me that my mother's choice of after-school apples was much better for us than the sweets offered at Amy's house.

"Look how slim you still are," Amy said. "You never packed on the saddlebags the way I did."

Trying to reason with her was pointless. Explaining our metabolism differences had never put a dent in Amy's comparisons of our body types. I weighed an easily camouflaged ten pounds more than I had weighed the day I graduated from high school. I never had carried a baby inside me for nine months, so I didn't personally appreciate the agony of extra pregnancy padding that wouldn't go away. Amy and I had different genetics. Straight and simple. But that line of reasoning never had gone over well with her, so I didn't resort to it now when she was in the midst of her weight management program.

In the first month she lost four pounds and was so motivated she talked me into joining an aerobics class with her. The best feature of this class was that it was for women over forty.

That sounded more appealing than the high-powered gym that offered free membership for the first month. Amy and I had visited that slick setup. We both left feeling intimidated and certain that we didn't want to try to negotiate a roomful of exercise machines in a coed gym. For one thing, we would have to buy new workout wardrobes to fit in with the other exercisers. Then we would have to go to a tanning booth and use some sort of super-whitening product on our teeth.

"I didn't see one person who looked like she *needed* to be working out at that gym," Amy said. "I'm going to find a place where we can blend in."

Extensive research efforts produced a lead on a place across town that was independently owned and for women only. We pulled up in front of the small strip mall before class on our first day, and I said, "So, where's the gym?"

"Right there."

"Where?" I saw a dry cleaner's, a dog wash, and a Vietnamese restaurant.

"It's that one." Amy pointed to the front door of a bright yellow store next to a vacuum cleaner repair shop. "See the sign? 'Lighten Up!'"

We entered the small sunshine yellow dance studio and joined a bunch of over-forty women who jumped and jiggled in chortling harmony. I have to admit it was fun. The music was lively. No one took the coordination of her moves too seriously. All that seemed to matter was that each of us moved something, somehow, and kept it moving until the end of the session.

Amy loved the class. Afterward, the glowing women stood in clumps, making plans for where they would go for tacos and diet colas.

The funniest woman in the class was Shirleene. She called all of us "girl." I became Lisa-girl and Amy was

Amy-girl. Shirleene had ample parts of her personage to jiggle, and yet she was by far the one who worked the hardest without ever moaning or showing a frown. Shirleene kept the rest of the group smilin' and groovin'—especially Amy.

On our second visit, Shirleene was standing behind us. Halfway through the second song she burst out, "Come on, Amy-girl, shake what yo' mama gave you!"

Amy ramped up her swish and wiggled like I'd never seen before. Not even when we used to dance in her bedroom with the door closed on Saturday morning and we listened to the countdown of the top ten on her transistor radio.

Every class from then on included Shirleene's prodding to "shake it," and every time, Amy did not disappoint.

I soon noticed that Shirleene never encouraged me to shake what my mama gave me. I think I knew why. My endowment for the art of shake, rattle, and roll was lacking. I was the underachiever in the class, noticeably deficient in the area of Motown moves.

One night, when Joel was gone, I found a radio station that played music like the tunes we danced to in our aerobics class. I cleared some space, pulled down all the shades, and took my position in front of the full-length bedroom mirror. Then I began my homework, hoping the extra credit might make up for some of my deficiencies in class.

What I witnessed in that mirror will long be etched in my psyche. Unfortunately. I felt pity for the other women in my class. I also felt thankful that we didn't exercise in front of any mirrors at the Lighten Up! studio. My skinny, white-girl body tried its best to shimmy up some R-E-S-P-E-C-T, but it just wasn't going to happen. Amy-girl could shake it with Aretha's songs as Shirleene's rolling laughter egged her on. I would forever be the aerobics class nerd.

But I kept at it each week in a show of support for Amy.

By the end of the third week, I weighed in seven pounds less than my starting weight. After a month I was eleven pounds lighter. Poor Amy had only lost two pounds. I knew I had to either fake some sort of injury that would keep me out of class for a few months or bulk up on chocolate malts.

I, of course, went with the chocolate malts. It worked great until Amy caught me. We were leaving the studio after class the first week of September. Usually we drove separately, but this time I was driving us both. I'd lost another pound that week, despite the chocolate malt. Amy hadn't lost even an ounce that week.

"I don't know why I bother." She sighed.

"Don't get discouraged. You know you've lost inches even if the pounds aren't showing up on the scale yet. You said your jeans feel looser. That should be encouraging."

"I know."

"And you're feeling healthier. The goal is to be healthy first, and then the weight comes off naturally. Isn't that what you've been telling me?"

"That's what I've been preaching. You know what? I should have taken off my jewelry before I got on the scale. This watch is at least four ounces. Maybe five. And what about these earrings?"

"Amy."

"No, I'm serious."

"In that case, did you shave your legs today?"

"No. I didn't!" Her face lit up with hope. "What a great idea! Next weigh-in I'll make sure I shave nice and close. I'll exhale before I step on the scale. And I won't wear an underwire bra that day. Hey, I could get my hair cut, too!"

"I was only kidding about shaving your legs. Don't get your hair cut. Your hair is perfect the way it is. Besides, your hair doesn't weigh a whole pound."

"It might. It's pretty thick. If I shaved all my hair off my head, I think it would weigh at least a pound. Maybe two pounds."

"Amelie Jeanette DuPree Rafferty."

She shot one of her innocent smirks in my direction. "What?"

"You are not going to shave your head, so drop that idea right now. You will have to go through the rest of your life never knowing how much your hair really weighs."

"You take all the fun out of everything," Amy muttered.

Without paying attention to where I was driving, I pulled into Jack in the Box, like I usually did, and heard what had become a familiar voice greet me through the speaker. I knew the regular employee could see my car in the round traffic mirror affixed to the top of the menu sign. "Welcome to Jack in the Box. The usual?"

"Ahh, no. Um. I'll have a diet soda. A small one. And ahh…do you want anything, Amy?"

"No."

"That's it. One small diet soda." I drove to the payment window with my eyes straight ahead.

"What did he mean by 'the usual'?" Amy asked.

"Hmm?"

"The guy just asked if you wanted the usual. I didn't know you had a usual at Jack in the Box."

I knew I had to come clean. I confessed, and Amy stared at me with her mouth open. I thought she was going to be mad. Very mad. Maybe angrier than she had ever been with me.

To my surprise, she started to laugh and couldn't stop. "You are such a sneak!" She swatted me on the arm as I pulled out money to pay for my diet soda. "I can't believe you!"

I drove home feeling ever so sheepish. Amy offered me the out I'd been hesitant to ask for. "Lisa, you don't have to do this anymore. I can do this on my own. I'm not going to quit if you don't go every week."

"I don't mind going. It's just that I'm not an aerobics kind of person," I said, still trying to build my defense.

Excuses were never required with Amy. She waved her hand. "Don't worry about it. You're under no obligation. You don't have to go to another workout with me ever, unless you want to."

"Are you sure?"

"Of course! If I ever need a ride, I'll call Shirleene."

I imagined Shirleene could get Amy to burn a couple hundred extra calories each week if they carpooled because she would have Amy laughing all the way to class and home.

"You know," Amy said, as I pulled up in front of her house, "I do appreciate your gesture, Lisa. I know you were sticking with me to keep me motivated. But honestly, you don't have to be that loyal to me. I'm sure psychologists with impressive degrees write books about people like you and me."

I relaxed. "That's okay; let them diagnose us. We've always known we were a little crazy."

"Just a little." Amy started to get out of the car and then turned back, eyeing my untouched diet soda. "You going to drink that?"

"I hate diet drinks."

"I know." Amy laughed at me again and snatched up the drink. "Brutally honest. Yes, that's the Lisa I know and love. Don't let that true Lisa get lost again in her kindness to me, okay?"

By Labor Day Amy had dropped a solid eight pounds. She sedately nibbled on the potato salad, hot dogs, and ice cream sandwiches the rest of us ate at our combined family end-of-summer BBQ. I'm sure I ate twice as much as she did and paid for it with a stomachache that night.

I could tell that after the past three months of adjusting her eating habits, Amy was on the road to success. Organic omega-3 eggs and cold-pressed flax seed oil were some of the secret ingredients found in her refrigerator at all times. I was impressed with her diligence.

At Thanksgiving, Amy wore a new pair of dress pants that were two sizes smaller than the others in her closet. For Christmas everyone gave her gift certificates so she could buy new clothes. While the rest of us sat around at a New Year's party at our house joking about our outlandish resolutions that we always listed but never kept, Amy only smiled. I knew she had smashed her glass ceiling on losing weight. The slow and easy approach allowed her the freedom to fully enjoy "a taste" of every Christmas goodie that came her way; yet she kept her metabolism working at an elevated level.

By Valentine's Day Amy and I were busy pulling together our travel plans. We had our airline tickets, hotel reservations, new wheelie suitcases, and more tour books on Paris than either of us had been able to read in our free time.

I was teaching third grade that year, which is why Amy

and I had set our travel dates to coincide with spring break. The substitute teacher I requested was a friend of mine. Even though I was only scheduled to miss a few days of class after we returned from Paris, I knew that if I was too tired to go back to work, I could leave the class in her capable hands for a full week after the trip.

Whenever we mentioned where we were going in April, people would invariably get this faraway look in their eyes and say, "Ah, springtime in Paris!" When we asked, almost all of them said they had never been to Paris, but if they were ever to go, they wanted to go in the spring.

Amy's anticipation for our pending adventure grew, but her biggest dilemma was shopping. She didn't want to buy new travel clothes until she lost those final few elusive pounds. The problem was she was running out of time to go shopping. I called her a week and a half before our departure date, and we made plans to shop on Saturday.

"The problem is I'm between sizes." Amy stepped out of a dressing room with two pairs of jeans in her hands. "I don't know if I should buy the ones that are a little too tight when I sit down or the ones that are a little too loose. I'm afraid that if I buy the loose jeans, I'll fill up the extra space with croissants."

"Buy both pairs," I suggested. "Wear the loose ones on the plane and other times when we're sitting all day. Then wear the tight ones when we're walking around because they won't feel tight, and they'll make you feel good about all the weight you've lost."

"You're a genius," Amy said, as we made our way to the cash register.

On the way home she asked if Joel was having any hesitancy about our trip.

"No. All along he's said that he hopes we have a good time. He did make one request that I haven't followed through on. He said we should buy travel insurance."

"Not a bad idea," Amy said. "I can work on that this week."

I forgot all about the insurance until the day we left for Paris. Mark drove Amy and me to the airport long before the break of day. As he loaded my wheeled suitcase into the back of their SUV, I noticed two other suitcases already in the open space.

"Are you going with us?" I teased Mark.

He nodded toward Amy, who was looking half apologetic in the front seat. "Those are both mine."

As I tumbled into the car, Amy explained how Mark had run out the night before and bought her another suitcase. "I was driving him crazy with my packing and unpacking. It's torture to be between sizes. Life was so much easier when everything in my closet was the same size. It was your suggestion that finally solved the problem."

"My suggestion?"

"With the jeans. You told me to buy both pairs, and I did. It suddenly made sense last night to pack two of everything. Now I won't get all the way over there and be bummed out because I can't manage to fit in the smaller clothes after a day of pastry tasting."

I had been to Europe before. Amy hadn't. She had only been on a few short plane trips, including the one their family took to Orlando when the kids were little. Amy was used to having Mark around to haul her luggage. I was nervous about how she was going to manage two suitcases as we moved through the airport and down cobblestone streets.

I blurted out, "You can only wear one thing at a time, you know. Trust me, comfort will win out over fashion every morning when you realize you'll be walking all over the place and not returning to the hotel until late at night."

"Lisa, last time you went you lived out of a backpack. You told me you only took two T-shirts for ten days."

"I took a few more this time."

"And so did I," Amy said with a flip in her voice.

Mark kept looking straight ahead and driving. He had seen us take our sparring positions before and knew better than to step in as a referee.

I looked out the window and reminded myself that this trip wasn't going to be like last time in any respect. This was Amy's turn to encounter Paris, and if she wanted to show up with two suitcases full of wardrobe options, who was I to shame her? She undoubtedly still had visions of making a debutante entrance.

We changed the subject and arrived at the airport in plenty of time. Acting as our valet, Mark toted both of Amy's suitcases into the terminal. She carried her purse and medium-sized carry-on bag while I easily maneuvered my compact pieces of baggage. Mark stayed with us until we had checked in for our flight and reached the security checkpoint.

As he kissed Amy good-bye, I wished Joel had come as well and was giving me a passionate send off, too. Joel had offered twice to come, but I had insisted that wasn't necessary. We had said our ardent good-byes the night before and left each other on sweet terms. Joel had asked that I bring him back some interesting sort of French food that would travel home well. I, of course, already was thinking chocolate.

That's when I secretly wished I'd brought two suitcases. It was going to be hard to pack a serious amount of the good stuff into my already full luggage. Maybe Amy did know more about making a trip to Paris than I did.

Five

Due to an electrical storm, our early flight was delayed. We waited in the boarding area for an hour and ten minutes before the announcement came that our flight was canceled. I'd never seen such a crazy scramble of frantic travelers.

Thanks to my aggressive advance through the terminal to the service desk, we were among the first to ask about rescheduling our flight. The airline employee studied our paperwork, checked our passports, and typed on the keyboard as if every key was sticking and needed extra coaxing to move. "We have a direct flight tomorrow morning at 8:10 that will get you into Paris at 9:20 tomorrow night."

"Nothing else going out today?" I asked.

"No."

"What about a flight with another airline?" Amy still

was breathing hard. "Who has a flight that goes out today?"

The woman tapped the keyboard again with renewed aggressiveness. "I'm showing two more flights today, but…" She tapped some more.

"We'll pay extra." Amy reached for her wallet.

"I'll need to see your tickets again."

Amy looked at me and said, "Ooh!"

"What?"

"I almost forgot. We have travel insurance! Here. What does our policy cover in a case like this?"

The woman looked perturbed. "I'll need to call a supervisor who can assist you with that."

A uniformed gentleman came out of the back area and clearly was not pleased to see Amy's "get out of jail free" card. He skimmed the forms and scowled at the computer screen.

"Okay," he said after a few seemingly effortless clicks. "Two for Charles de Gaulle Airport departing from gate 83 in one hour."

"Thank you," Amy and I said in unison.

"And," he lowered his voice, as if it was particularly painful for him to announce this final adjustment. "Both of your seats are in first class."

Amy and I scooted to our gate, settled into our wide reclining leather seats, and shared a quiet giggle.

"This is so cool!" Amy said. "Let's hear it for Joel's insistence that we buy travel insurance including upgrades on the next available flight!"

I felt proud of my husband at that moment.

Our flight attendant offered to take our coats and hang them up. He then offered us orange juice, which was served in glass tumblers. Amy and I clinked the rims of our glasses in a toast, and Amy said, "Oh, taste and see that the LORD is good."

It seemed an odd choice for an orange juice toast. As soon as I got the pulp out of my teeth, I asked, "Did you just make that one up?"

"That one what?"

"That toast about tasting to see that the Lord is good."

"No, it's a verse. In Psalms."

"I thought it sounded familiar."

Amy leaned closer. "I've been working on a sort of secret project."

"You have? Something other than this trip?"

She nodded. "I'm collecting verses that have to do with adjusting my eating habits. I've memorized some of them, and I'm thinking of having them printed up on little cards or maybe made into posters. Shirleene said I should have them made into refrigerator magnets. She said some of them would act like a stop sign whenever a person went after something in the fridge she shouldn't be eating."

I'd never noticed verses that had to do with eating habits in the Bible. But then, I'd never looked for them.

"What are they?"

"Do you mean what are the verses?"

"Yeah, I want to hear some of them. You've got my curiosity going."

Amy looked as if she was blushing a little. "Okay, first you have to keep in mind that they're supposed to be for encouragement, and they're not all supposed to be taken literally."

"That's okay. Go ahead, tell me some of them. I want to hear."

"Okay. Well, there's Isaiah 55:2, 'Listen, listen to me, and eat what is good.'"

"That's a good one," I said. "Especially the 'eat what is good' part."

"Right. Okay. And then Proverbs 16:24, 'Pleasant words are a honeycomb, sweet to the soul and healing to the bones.'"

"Very nice."

"Then there's Shirleene's favorite. Actually, she's the one who got me started in looking up these verses, because she told me that Leviticus 3:16 was her life verse."

"Her life verse? From Leviticus 3:16? Are you sure she didn't mean John 3:16?"

"No, it's Leviticus 3:16. I'm sure."

"So what is it?"

Amy hesitated, as if she had to explain to me that Shirleene said or did things out of the ordinary.

"Come on, Amy. I know Shirleene. I can take it."

Amy grinned. "Okay, here it is. 'All the fat is the LORD's.'"

I covered my face with my hand and kept my chuckle inside. I could just hear Shirleene delivering her line in aerobics class, rallying the others the same way she did with her, "Shake what yo' mama gave you!" line.

"I looked it up," Amy said, defending Shirleene's choice. "The chapter is about sacrifices. I told Shirleene that, and she said we're supposed to be living sacrifices. So when we get burned up ounce by ounce, it means that all the fat can very well belong to the Lord. It's our own little praise offering to Him."

I grinned at Amy, letting her know she didn't have to worry about offending me. Her explanation was honest and delivered without any disrespect for the great God in heaven whom I knew she honored.

With a tip of my orange juice tumbler in her direction, I leaned back into the cushiness of first class. "I'm not my mother, Amy. You can quote any verse you want to me at any time, and I will be happy to hear it."

Amy lowered her chin. "Then I guess I should tell you my personal favorite."

"I'm all ears."

"It's Revelation 3:2."

"Ah, an end-times verse!" I said, knowing that as the last book in the Bible, Revelation carried all kinds of passages that were subject to a variety of interpretations on how the world was going to end. Perhaps Amy's verse also was open to an assortment of interpretations.

"Actually, it's more of a midlife verse that applies to a woman like me who started to lose weight and suddenly finds she's lacking in the muscle-tone department." Amy lifted her arm and jiggled her underarm flab for emphasis. "The verse says, 'Wake up! Strengthen what remains.'"

This time I laughed aloud. Amy smiled winsomely. I wondered what God thought of Amy at moments like this. Somehow I had a feeling she made Him smile.

I often found myself thinking the way to find favor with God was through the obedience school of my childhood training. Every verse of Scripture and every theological premise had to be understood flawlessly before I could discuss it with others. Amy, however, seemed to revel in the access she had to all that was sacred. She loved exploring the depths of truth in all its possible forms. I wondered if she was one of those children who continually brought a twinkle to God's ever-watchful eye.

I had a feeling Amy was in line for plenty of blessings before this trip was over, and I didn't mind absorbing any excess. Especially when that excess started with a flight over the Atlantic Ocean while reclining in first class with soft pillows and cozy lap quilts. We even were offered small printed menus listing our options for meal service. Menus!

Our beef Stroganoff was served with warm dinner rolls

and white cloth napkins. The nest of fresh greens came with juicy mandarin orange slices and caramelized walnuts.

After the most luxurious flight either of us had ever experienced, Amy and I landed in Paris and were herded efficiently through customs. We collected our luggage without a snag. I watched Amy devise a piggyback system with a strap on her luggage so she could pull the pieces behind her like a train.

"I'm impressed."

"You better be," she answered with a wry grin.

As we navigated our way through the airport, aside from the overhead announcements being delivered to us in French, nothing yet seemed extraordinary. But Amy's expression showed that she found everything happening around her magical.

"That guy back there just told the woman that their flight to Milan was delayed."

I kept walking, expecting Amy to explain why that was relevant.

She looked over to the side and then said, "Those two girls with the cell phones are mad at their friend because she didn't call them yet."

I realized what was happening. Amy was eavesdropping on the sea of French conversations while I ignorantly sailed by all the same people without a clue as to what they were saying. I began to grasp what an advantage Amy's familiarity with the French language was going to be.

"Do you know which one of these signs directs us to the taxi stand?" I asked.

Amy looked up. "Sure. It's that one."

I followed her out into the night air and told her how much I was going to appreciate her translation skills.

"I hope I can come up with enough French words to tell the driver the name of our hotel," Amy said.

"If we have any problems, we can just show him the paper with the printed-out reservation."

"Did you take taxis a lot the last time you were here?"

"No. I don't remember ever taking a cab in Paris. We were seeing Europe on ten dollars a day. That meant a lot of walking and taking the bus or the Metro. Not taxis."

Amy and I moved to the front of the line with our luggage, and as the next black sedan taxi pulled up, Amy said, "Check out the license! It looks like a subliminal ad for the flax seed oil I use."

I squinted through my glasses and read the numbers: 050FLX50.

That was my first clue that Amy might be experiencing jet lag. She was seeing word puzzles in license plates.

The driver hopped out and quickly stuffed our bags into the ample trunk before running around to his door and taking off into the airport traffic with a bolt.

"Hotel Isabella, *s'il vous plaît*," Amy said, sounding eager to try out her French. "Hotel Isabella," the driver responded. "Oui."

I discreetly put my finger to my lips as a signal to Amy not to say anything that might give away her accent. A lot of my former travel survival techniques were coming back to me. In some countries, we found we were treated better if it wasn't obvious we were Americans. If Amy and I chatted away in English with American accents, I knew we possibly could be charged more than, say, a German tourist.

Amy trusted my subtle signal and kept quiet until the driver asked us something in rapid French. Amy calmly responded.

That was okay. The goof-up was that as soon as she responded to him, she turned to translate for me. Just as she had done for years whenever I didn't understand Grandmere.

"He said our hotel is close to the Louvre. We should ask for a room facing the Jardin des Tuileries—the park— then we'll be able to see the Eiffel Tower."

Glancing at me in the rearview mirror, the driver narrowed his eyes. "American?"

I wished at that moment that I spoke another language. Any language. I would have settled for a Canadian passport, even, to hold up for him to see.

But I was taught never to lie. "Yes. Oui. American."

I was sure we were doomed. Yet the words that came from our driver's mouth startled me. "*C'est bon!* Do you okay eef I practeece English for you?"

"Sure!" Amy said. "Oui."

"I show to you zee home of Voltaire, our famous philosopher and French writer."

"Is it on the way to our hotel?" I asked.

"Oui. Yes, yes."

He was driving on to a city street, and all around us were tall old stone buildings. I hadn't gotten my bearings to know what part of Paris proper we were entering. Then I saw the familiar spiral of light in the distance on our left. Actually, Amy saw it first.

"The Eiffel Tower! Look, it's all lit up! Ooh, it's beautiful!"

"Theese is your first veezit to Paris?"

"Yes," Amy said. "My friend has been here before, but this is my first time."

"You must have chocolat to drink at Angelina's. Right by your hotel. Very good chocolat. And Sacré Coeur. This you must see in Montmartre." He went on listing all of his personal favorites of this great city and warmed up to his use of English by giving bits of history about various buildings as we sped past them in the dark.

"Voilá! The home of Voltaire. This corner. Up. You see?"

We saw an ornate building, like the many other ornate buildings we had been rolling past for several blocks. I didn't know exactly what we should have been looking for to see where Voltaire lived.

"And zee Louvre." He pointed to the enormous U-shaped continuation of buildings on the right. The glass pyramid entrance had been added since I had visited last. Lit up in the center of the commons, the pyramid gave Napoleon's former palace grounds a strange Star Trekkiness.

Our chatty driver turned left on the Rue de Rivoli and suddenly stopped the car in the lane of traffic closest to the covered sidewalk. "Hotel Isabella," he announced. Cars honked and swerved around us.

"Do you take credit cards?" Amy asked. "Visa?"

"No, sorry. Cash only." He pointed to the digital meter that read 78.25.

"Seventy-eight euros?" Amy asked, as the two of us fumbled for our wallets. We had been so caught up in the tour we weren't prepared to exit the taxi. "Do you have change for a hundred?"

"No, sorry."

I fiddled with the bills in my wallet, trying to see in the dark. "Here's a fifty. I think that's a fifty. What do you have, Amy?"

"Nothing small. Here." She held out one of her hundred-euro bills. "Keep the change."

I gave Amy a hard look, but I don't think she caught my expression in the dark. It wasn't a good idea to begin our journey with such generosity.

"Thank you. Thank you."

Amy patted him on the arm and said something in French. He reached for her hand and kissed it twice, gushing a line or two in French that I'm sure were very suave.

Amy giggled, scooted out of the backseat after me, and waved as the smooth operator zoomed off into the traffic. We dashed for the sidewalk before the oncoming cars rolled over us.

"Ooh, the French," Amy said, as the hotel doors automatically opened. "That was memorable. Wasn't he charming?"

"Charming." I made sure the word came out as flat as I felt. It was pointless now to comment on the excessive tip. We were here. That was all that mattered.

Stepping into the unexpectedly compact hotel lobby, I felt another dip. I hoped our rooms weren't as small and as economically decorated.

A young man in a red vest and white shirt with a bow tie welcomed us in French to the Hotel Isabella. He seemed to be the only one working the night shift.

"Merci." Amy pulled out her reservations paper. With a few clumsy French sentences, she asked if our room faced the Jardin des Tuileries. It didn't, but the clerk switched to speaking English and graciously made the room change for us. Amy kept grinning, whispering to me that, thanks to our terrific cab driver's advice, we would now see the Eiffel Tower from our room.

All I wanted to see was the front end of a steak sandwich as it entered my mouth and then a nice bed to flop in.

"Would you like assistance with your luggage?" the desk clerk asked.

Our luggage?

Amy and I froze.

Six

Our luggage!

"Our suitcases are still in the cab!" Amy squeaked.

"We have to call the taxi company immediately," I demanded. "And the police. That driver took off with our luggage!"

The desk clerk made a quick phone call and turned to us for more information. "Did your driver give you a receipt?"

"No."

"No receipt? No business card?"

We shook our heads.

He gave us a wary look, spoke a few more words to the person on the other end of the phone, and hung up. With his palms turned toward us he said, "Without identification, it is not possible to know which taxi or car service brought you to the hotel. Sorry."

Amy and I looked at each other desperately.

"There has to be some way…" I began.

"Wait!" Amy clapped her hands and spurted out, "050FLX50! That was his license plate. I remember it; I thought it was an ad for flax seed oil."

The hotel clerk looked amused at Amy's clever little talent.

"Are you sure?" he asked.

"Oui! *Positif!*" Amy picked up a pen and wrote the number on a brochure about Versailles.

He picked up the phone again and made several more calls for us, this time speaking in crisp authoritative French. I stood unmoving, clenching my jaw. Amy pressed her lips together and fidgeted.

It took far too long before the clerk hung up the phone. "The information I have for you is not so good. The police would like for you to go to the *commissariat* to file a report."

"The police station?" Amy said. "Why? Can't the taxi company call the driver and ask him to come back?"

"In a normal problem, yes, it is possible. However, this is not a normal problem." His expression turned curiously sympathetic. "You are certain of this license number?"

"Positive," Amy said. "Positif."

"Then you have a problem. The taxi company says the car you were in was stolen two weeks ago. The police concur. They have not been able to find the taxi."

"Are you saying a crazy guy is driving around Paris picking up people in a stolen taxi?" Amy asked.

"Oui."

"I don't believe this." I felt a sudden need to sit down. Instead, I grasped the corner of the front desk. "That man is driving around, charging people way too much money for cab fare and stealing their luggage. And you're saying that in the past two weeks no one has been able to stop him?"

"*Exactement.*"

"I can't believe this!"

"I can make for you a map to the commissariat," the hotel clerk said.

"Is it far to walk?" Amy asked. "Because we're not taking a taxi."

"No, not far."

As much as I didn't want to walk anywhere, I knew neither of us would be able to sleep until we had done all we could to retrieve our luggage.

The clerk handed Amy the map along with the keys to our hotel room. We stomped out of the hotel's automatic door with our arms linked and our purses smashed in between us for added theft protection from sidewalk hooligans.

Our march down the Rue de Rivoli seemed safe enough. Then we turned left at the first narrow side street. The uneven pavement took us past a small convenience store.

"I need some water," Amy said. "I'm feeling really woozy."

Entering the small store, Amy greeted the swarthy man behind the register. He was looking at a magazine with a naked woman on the cover.

"Come on." I nudged her back out of the store. "Let's keep going. We can get water at the police station."

"What are you doing?" Amy protested, as I took her arm and pulled her onward.

"What were you doing, trying to start a conversation with that guy?"

"I was being polite. You know, manners? Grandmere taught me a long time ago that when you're in Paris you're supposed to greet the shop people and say good-bye when you leave. That's the Parisian way."

"Amy, that may have applied when your grandmere lived here, but if you start being polite to every unsavory sort of character in Paris, you're going to be sorry."

She looked at me as if I were crazy. "Okay, fine. Let's just find the police station."

We forged ahead a few more blocks. The exercise and cool air gave us both a chance to calm down. Turning a corner, we came into an open square encompassed by old stone buildings that looked as though they hadn't changed for several hundred years. I could almost picture the window shutters on the second story of one of the houses opening up and a maid tossing out a bucket of vegetable peels.

"Look at this!" Amy stopped and took in the slice of Parisian life.

On the corner, accordion music danced its way from under a gathering of café umbrellas looped with twinkle lights. At nearly every table relaxed groups of people sat talking and drinking wine from rounded goblets. A man in a business suit arrived at the café on a Vespa-style motor scooter and parked in front. The streets were too narrow for cars, but plenty of locals were out walking, even though it was past ten o'clock.

"It looks like a movie set." Amy gazed across the open square to the gathering of human moths fluttering around the flickering lights.

I had to agree. It was magical.

"Look at how happy those people are," Amy said.

"Yeah, well, that's because they're putting food in their mouths, and better still, all of them know where their next change of clean underwear is coming from."

"Lisa, who cares about underwear at a time like this? Don't you just want to go over there and start our introduction to Paris all over again?"

I was too numb to answer.

"I do," she said. "I want to sit at that café with all those French people. I want to eat something deliciously French and listen to them speaking French."

I wanted to cry. I wanted to sit on that cobblestone street and burst into tears and get it over with. I was too tired, too hungry, and too angry about our stolen luggage to entertain Amy's dreamy reflections. Using my firmest, nonnegotiable voice, I said, "Amy, we have to file the police report. We can come back and have a leisurely dinner later."

She sighed, as if the enchanting slice of behind-the-scenes Paris was beginning to evaporate like a mythical Brigadoon and wouldn't appear for another hundred years. "You're right." She fell in step beside me.

We wove our way down another narrow street lined with what looked like front doors to dozens of homes where the lights were off for the evening.

"You know what?" Amy stopped at the corner next to a closed bookshop. "I just realized something. We haven't prayed yet. God knows where our luggage is. He can direct that driver to come back to the hotel and return our suitcases. Let's ask Him to do that."

I wanted to say, "Oh, come on, Amy. We shouldn't bother God with our mess. He's probably as tired and frustrated as we are. Let's just keep going and take care of this ourselves."

But she started to pray before I could protest. Without closing her eyes, Amy took a deep breath. "Papa, You know everything. You know where our suitcases are right now, and You know that taxi driver even if He doesn't know You. You can do anything. If You want to get our luggage back, You can make that happen. If You want us to go without our things so we can trust You in new ways, that's okay, too. May Your kingdom come and Your will be done on earth as it is in heaven. Amen."

Amy smiled at me, and I found a small smile inside my quieted heart to give back to her. It was a good thing she was the one who prayed instead of me. My prayer would have come out a little more…well, aggressive.

Years ago when I heard Amy address God in prayer as Papa, I had questioned her. The term didn't seem appropriate or honoring. But then I was still reading only the King James Version of the Bible with all the *thee* and *thou* phrases I'd grown up hearing in church.

"Calling on God as my Papa changes everything for me," Amy had told me soon after she discovered the Romans 8 reference to *Abba Father* could be translated to mean "Papa" or "Daddy" in English. "Don't you see? I never had a relationship with my earthly father, so it always was difficult for me to picture my heavenly Father as being there for me or wanting to love me. But when I saw God as my Papa, I felt I could trust Him and come close to Him any time, and He would never desert me."

I knew that everything Amy said to her heavenly Papa in prayer she meant. She trusted and adored God in a way I'd never been able to grasp. She believed her heavenly Papa could direct the heart of a Parisian car thief to turn around and return our stolen luggage. Her simple faith humbled me. Especially because she believed enough for both of us.

The irony was that even though I was the one who gave Amy her first Bible, she was the one who continually gave the Bible back to me every time the truths of God's Word came springing out in her life like a fountain of fresh water. Whenever they did, I drank deeply, unaware until that moment how desperately thirsty I was.

Continuing on our trek to the police station, I forgot how hungry, tired, and angry I was. We studied the hand-drawn map together and turned right at the next corner.

"There it is. On the right." Amy led the way down the narrow street lined with small parked cars.

Entering the unassuming police station, I felt as if we were entering a parallel universe to *The Andy Griffith Show* but with some peculiar twists. The two officers on duty were watching *The Simpsons* on a small television with the volume turned low. One of them was smoking. He immediately put his cigarette behind his back, as if one of us were his mother and had stepped into his bedroom unannounced.

Both of the men stood up straight to greet us in their freshly pressed uniforms. They couldn't have been much older than twenty.

Amy explained our problem in chopped-up French. She added a stream of apologies in English for all the words she couldn't remember. Then she apparently asked for something to drink.

The officers responded immediately. The shorter one

pulled a bottle of wine out of the desk drawer and went looking for glasses.

Amy called after him in French requesting water.

The other officer reached for a pad of paper and asked Amy a string of questions. She tried to keep up with the translation for me, explaining that the men had received the dispatch of our situation and needed more details from us.

Two glasses of lukewarm water were offered to us, and I discreetly didn't drink mine. I doubted it was bottled water, and I didn't want to get sick my first night here.

Amy tried to explain the questions the officer was asking her.

"Amy, don't worry about translating for me. You can just answer everything so that things go faster."

If these young men spoke English, they weren't planning to use it. Instead, they tested Amy's weary French vocabulary to its limits. I was proud of her. She kept on task and tried hard to communicate.

I wished I could have been some help. The shorter officer bounced between listening to Amy's descriptions and trying to engage me in the conversation. I did a lot of sideways nodding, trying to get him to pay attention to Amy. My stomach grumbled loudly at one point, and I placed my hand over it as if to silence it. The officer asked me something, and Amy said he was offering us food.

"That's okay." I held up my hand to let him know I was okay. "We can eat later."

Amy looked at me and then at the officer. She spoke to him, and with a nod he slipped out the front door.

"What did you say?"

"I told him we were hungry."

"Amy, he doesn't have to feed us."

"It's okay. Relax."

I was not at all relaxed as I saw the young man take off on a Vespa and putter down the narrow street. He returned less than five minutes later with a long loaf of French bread tucked under his arm. Entering the station, he held up the bread and a small bag of Roma tomatoes and said something to Amy.

"He went to his apartment," Amy said. "That was nice of him. Merci."

I watched him slice the crusty bread with a pocketknife and hold out a chunk for me on the tip of the blade. My first thoughts were, "I don't want the section of bread that was under his armpit," followed by, "I hope he washed those tomatoes." Then I realized what a germ-freak I was being. Growing up I had eaten everything placed before me.

"Merci." I received the gift that was being offered so sincerely. Something inside me stepped down a notch in that moment. I was a guest in a foreign country. Practically a refugee, since we were without luggage. I should just be quiet and be appreciative.

The dry bread and ripe tomatoes were nice. Tasty, even.

Half an hour later Amy finished providing the men with all the particulars. Paperwork completed, she told them in English and then again in French where we could be reached if any news came in about the taxi or our luggage.

The men smiled for the first time that night, and one of them said something to Amy that made her blush. She smiled and shook her head saying no and thanking him. I thought I noticed a hint of tears glistening in her eyes. As soon as we were out of the station, I asked Amy what he had said.

"He offered us a ride back to the hotel on his Vespa," she said with a crooked grin. "But he could only take us one at a time, so I declined."

"Good choice. Not that I wasn't secretly hoping you would leave me at the police station while you took off scooting about Paris with your arms around the middle of a man young enough to be your son."

Amy started to cry.

"I was only teasing, Amy."

"I know. And what you just said was hilarious." She propped open a wobbly, upside-down umbrella smile that caught her spring shower of tears.

"Then why are you crying?"

"Because for that brief moment I believed I actually could fit on the back of a Vespa!"

"Of course you could fit on the back of a Vespa. In your skinny jeans, no less!"

Amy's shower of tears turned into a downpour.

"What? Amy, what's wrong?"

"My skinny jeans are in our stolen luggage!" she wailed.

Seven

I fumbled in my shoulder bag for a tissue and handed it to Amy under the glow of the streetlight. "It's been a long day. We'll go shopping tomorrow and buy you some new skinny jeans. Shopping in Paris! Ooh la la, right? How fun will that be?"

"Lisa, it's not the jeans. It's more than that." She sniffed. "Don't you see? We're in Paris. It's spring. Springtime in Paris! You and I are finally here. A French guy just offered me a ride on the back of his Vespa!"

"Yes," I said, still not seeing the cause for so much emotion.

"A year ago if someone would have made me an offer like that I would have thought they were making fun of me!" She burst into a fresh round of tears.

"Oh, Amy-girl!" I wrapped my arms around her. "You

did a superb job losing all that weight. You should be flattered that he offered you a ride."

"I am flattered." She pulled back and wiped her tears. "That's just it, Lisa. Don't you see?"

I was having a hard time seeing anything through my hazy brain at that moment. I handed her another tissue. Amy blew her nose and dabbed away the final tears. "This is what I always dreamed of you and me doing."

"What, blowing your nose at midnight on a Paris street corner?"

"No, being here. Together. Coming to Paris. We did it! We're here! But I didn't expect to be this old when we finally showed up. Don't you see? We're here, but we're old. It's all so wonderful and so tragic at the same time."

"I know." I gave her my most sympathetic smile. But I knew something Amy didn't. Age had nothing to do with the aching that had overtaken my forty-five-year-old friend. Paris was equally exhilarating and tragic when I was twenty-two.

I said, "There's something about this city that breaks your hope into a thousand pieces and then stands back and watches as you cut yourself trying to gather up the shards."

"Ooh," Amy said pensively.

"Yeah. Ooh or ow, whichever the case may be. Come on." I put my arm around Amy's shoulders. "We'll both feel better after we get something else to eat and get some sleep. Why don't we walk across the cobblestones, sit down at that café, and order some food?"

"I'm too tired to try to order in French. I think I've used up every French word I know."

With no decision-making skills between the two of us, Amy and I ended up back at the creepy convenience store where we ignored the brooding man at the register. We left with bottled water and two oranges. We also bought contact lens solution for Amy, toothbrushes and toothpaste, and what we hoped was roll-on deodorant. It was either deodorant or a spot remover for clothing. At that point, we didn't care.

As we entered the hotel, the night desk clerk politely greeted us and asked if we met with success at the police station.

"No," Amy told him.

He didn't look too surprised, which was not very encouraging.

We rode the tiny elevator to our fourth-floor room in silence. At least the room was a nice size, and the twin beds looked inviting. I ate my orange and brushed my teeth with the chalky toothpaste.

"I miss my things." Amy sat on the edge of her bed, rubbing her bare feet. "I wouldn't make a very good player on *Survivor*." She finished her orange and then went into the bathroom to wash up.

"What am I going to do with my contacts?" she moaned.

"At home the travel boxes of solution come with a lens case. This one doesn't. Why is everything so complicated?"

"Amy, just put them in the drinking glasses and get some sleep. We'll figure all this out in the morning when we can think straight."

We turned out the light without a kind word between us and fell asleep in our clothes.

When I woke, it was daylight, but I refused to open my eyes. I had been dreaming I was in a Jerry Lewis sort of movie that took place at a sidewalk café lit up in twinkle lights. A bunch of Johnny Depps in dark-rimmed glasses were racing around on Vespas. Amy was waving to me from the back of one of the scooters that I think was being motored about by Michael Nesmith, the tall Monkee with the stocking cap. A uniformed police officer stood in the middle of a busy intersection holding up a white-gloved hand and blowing a whistle. I didn't know what people were saying in my dream because oddly, or perhaps expectedly, the dream was in nonsensical French phrases.

I drifted in that floaty, subconscious place between sleep cycles until Amy stirred in her bed. She padded over to the window, opened the drapes, and gasped. "Lisa, get up. You have to see this."

"I can see from here." I squinted in the daylight that now flooded our room. "What time is it?"

"Ten o'clock. And it's a beautiful day in Paris! Come over here."

I pulled my glasses off the bedside table and shuffled to the window. "Wow," I murmured with appreciation for the expansive garden that paralleled our hotel. The green grass and trees stretched as far as we could see from the Louvre to the Concorde. Below our window and across the street were a large Ferris wheel and other amusement park attractions. Behind the wide park rose the immense central train station making a bold statement. To our right in the distance stood the landmark known around the world. The Eiffel Tower.

"What a view!" Amy said.

"We didn't have a view like this from the youth hostel, I'll tell you that. What I remember the most about the youth hostel was how the common washroom had one long sink like a metal feeding trough. A long pipe ran above the trough. It was peppered with pinholes from which the cold water sprayed out. That was our only way to wash up. We had to go to a public bathhouse to shower."

"I don't imagine the beds were as nice, either," Amy said. "These beds are great. How did you sleep?"

I told her about my wacky dream and the part about Johnny Depp. She laughed. "Wait. Don't make me laugh any more. I have to go to the bathroom."

As I stood by the window and took in the view, Amy scooted into the bathroom.

"No!" Amy suddenly screeched.

"What? What's wrong?" I tapped on the closed bathroom door.

Amy opened it with a drinking glass in her hand. "I am such a doof."

"What happened?"

"I just drank my contact."

"Amy!"

"I know. Don't say anything. I know." She walked past me and crawled back into bed, putting the empty glass on the end table.

"You brought another pair of contact lenses, right?"

"Yes. Two pairs."

"And your glasses?"

"Of course."

"So, relax. I doubt the lens you swallowed will goof up your digestive system. Just drink some of your cranberry extract and psyllium stuff. You brought that, too, didn't you?"

"Yes, I brought some psyllium."

"See? You'll be fine."

Without looking at me, she pulled the covers up to her chin. "The psyllium is with my other pair of contacts, which are with my glasses."

That's when I knew what she was going to say next.

"And they're all together, packed neatly in my suitcase. My suitcase that is roaming around Paris in the trunk of a stolen taxi. "

"Oh, Amy."

"What was I thinking? Those are essential items. I should have put all of them in my purse. I don't know how to travel! I'm a train wreck, Lisa. A disaster limping from one fiasco to another!"

"No, you're not. We'll work this out. We'll find an optometrist or have Mark send some of your contacts or something."

"And what am I supposed to do in the meantime? Put in my one surviving contact and walk around viewing Paris with my other eye closed?"

"We could get an eye patch for you at a pharmacy," I said, halfway serious.

"Oh, great! How cute would that look? Can you see me showing up at the house Grandmere wanted me to visit? 'Hi, I'm Amy the Pirate, and yes, I have been wearing these same clothes for the past four days. But hey, at least you can't see the bruises on the back of my legs from when I *did* have luggage to haul around.'"

I ignored her ranting and stepped over to the phone.

"What are you doing?"

"Calling room service. We need some serious croissants and black coffee in here."

"Oh, sure. Try to cheer me up with food."

"Hey, I'm starving even if you aren't. *Bon jour*," I said, responding to the voice on the phone. "I would like to order some breakfast."

Even though I'd spoken my request slowly and assumed a large hotel like this would host English-speaking guests frequently, the woman's voice on the other end responded to me in French.

"I'm sorry, I…"

"Here." Amy reached for the phone. "*Pardon?*" she said and then followed with several smooth sentences in which the only word I recognized was *croissants*.

"Twenty-five minutes." Amy handed the phone back to me. "I hope you don't mind waiting that long."

"If I feel faint, I'll go drink your other contact."

Amy squinted her eyes. "You're just asking for it, Lisa-girl. I've never taken you out before, but I could do it right here, right now, if I had to."

Not since junior high school had I seen Amy go through so many mood swings in such a short period of time. It was as if this were her first time away from home and away from anyone who expected her to act a certain way. She seemed to be spinning through all the options, trying to decide if she was going to be tough chick Amy-girl or Amelie, American princess abroad.

Secretly, I enjoyed watching her find herself out of her element. I suspected I was seeing the true Amy, in all her variations.

"I dare ya." I challenged her to get out from under those puffy covers and prove to me she was brazen enough to start a catfight. It was a crazy way to begin our first day in Paris, but somehow, after all we'd been through, it didn't seem unreasonable.

"No," she said with a pout. "I'm going back to sleep. Wake me when the food arrives."

I was about to taunt her with some sort of sassy comeback when someone knocked on our door. Amy and I exchanged surprised glances. It was too soon for room service.

A knock sounded again. A male voice called out something in French. Amy's eyes widened. She hopped out of bed and stood behind the closed door, peeking through the small viewing hole. "Oui?"

"Who is it?" I asked.

"The hotel manager. He says there's an inspector in the lobby who wants to ask us some questions."

The manager spoke again through the closed door. Amy turned to me. "He wants to know if we're dressed and can go down to the lobby with him."

Sadly, we already were dressed and had no other apparel options.

"Oui," she answered the manager. In English she added, "We'll be right down." She repeated the phrase in French as I stepped into the bathroom and splashed some water on my face.

"I'm not going to put in my one contact," Amy said. "So if we need to read any fine print or sign anything, you'll have to do it for me."

I didn't explore the thought that my trying to read French fine print to her was not going to happen. Especially on an empty stomach. All I said was, "I hope this doesn't take very long. I don't want to miss breakfast when it shows up."

The uniformed inspector was all business. He stood to the side of the front desk, his hands clasped behind his back. He was nothing like the traffic-directing policeman in my dream the night before. And, as an added reality check, not a single Monkee popped out from behind the counter or rode a tricycle through the lobby.

"Bon jour," the inspector said without smiling.

"Bon jour," Amy and I repeated in unison.

He motioned for us to be seated on the only sofa and chair situated in the small lobby area. We were barely settled in before he asked us a question. Amy took it from there. Every so often she turned to me and asked for verification. Did the driver have dark hair? How tall would we estimate he was? Any distinguishing marks?

"I thought we went over all this last night," I said to Amy, while nodding politely to the inspector.

"No. The questions last night were about the taxi and where the driver picked us up."

The inspector took notes on a small pad of paper with a Montblanc pen. I noticed his long fingers and trim nails. His watch was gold and shaped like a rectangle. It was too bad I hadn't noticed as many details about our driver last night.

While Amy was nodding in response to one of the questions, I looked out the glass doors and noticed a taxi double-parked in front of the hotel. Two more taxis went around the idling car. I tried to imagine how many hundreds of taxis were driving around this huge city. Another taxi sped around the parked one, and I felt a new empathy for the police and their challenge of finding our contraband cab among perhaps thousands.

The automatic doors opened, and a dark-haired taxi driver entered pulling two wheeled suitcases behind him. He left a third suitcase outside on the curb. With my new powers of observation warming up, I noticed that he was wearing a gray sweater, but his head was down so I couldn't see his face. And no passengers were exiting the taxi. The luggage was being delivered sans hotel guests. A dozen reasons could explain such a drop-off, but the instant I spotted Amy's bright yellow luggage tags dangling from the otherwise nondescript black bags, I screamed.

Jumping to my feet, I charged toward the cabbie yelling, "Hey, you! What are you doing? Stop!"

He bolted, entered the taxi through the passenger side, and peeled out into the flow of traffic. An immediate chorus of honking from the other cars accompanied his getaway.

The inspector looked at me and then at Amy. She was rattling a string of words in French as I ran outside and grabbed what turned out to be my suitcase from the sidewalk where the cabbie had left it. I dashed back inside.

Amy was holding on to one of her luggage tags and nodding wildly.

With one swift motion, the inspector stormed the front desk, commandeered the telephone out of the hand of the dazed desk clerk, punched in some numbers, and barked orders. Three other hotel personnel appeared from a back room just as an older German-speaking couple exited the elevator. Everyone talked at once while the inspector shouted over the commotion.

Amy and I looked at each other open mouthed. A smile of uncontrollable exuberance lit up Amy's face. We both laughed.

I didn't want to be the doubting Thomas, but this was too bizarre. Too good to be true. I hurried to open my suitcase and immediately saw that all my neatly packed belongings had been rifled through.

"Amy, don't get too excited yet."

She sifted through her suitcase and pulled out a small slip of orange paper. "Hey, did you get one of these?"

Typed in English was a notice that U.S. Customs had searched her luggage as part of a routine security check. Spotting a matching orange card in my muddle of clothes, I withdrew my unbelief.

"Yes, my luggage was inspected, too."

"See!" Amy still was giggling. "God sent the thief back here this morning with our luggage. Isn't that a scream? Who says God doesn't answer prayer?"

Just then the inspector darted past us and ran out to the squad car that had pulled up in front of the hotel. The chase was on.

"Ooh! Don't you just want to go follow them?" Amy asked.

"Ah, no." I zipped up my suitcase.

"Come on, Lisa! Where's your sense of adventure?"

I couldn't help but laugh at Amy. "You know, as tempting as it sounds to go running around more unfamiliar streets in Paris in pursuit of a deranged taxi driver who demonstrated a strange sense of propriety in returning our belongings, I think I'd rather go upstairs and see if our breakfast has been delivered. Then I'd prefer to take a long hot shower and change clothes. To be honest."

"Well, I do always want you to be honest," Amy said, still smiling.

We rolled our luggage into the elevator, and Amy said, "Can you believe this? We asked God to bring our luggage to us, and He did."

Something inside me felt compelled to launch into a clarification of how prayer works. It seemed important to point out that God doesn't have to do what we ask, just because we cry out to Him whenever we have a problem. Things don't always go the way we think they should. This time it just happened to turn out favorably for us.

Then I realized I didn't have to explain God to Amy. Why was I trying to protect His reputation? All Amy wanted was to be delighted with what He had done.

She stood in the elevator beside me, lifting up her chin all the way and with a wide smile whispering, "Thank You, Papa! You are incredible! Thank You! Thank You! Thank You!"

I nodded my agreement with Amy in much the same way I'd passively acknowledged her prayer on the street corner last night. She was the one having all the fun and all the joy, celebrating the three little lost sheep that had come back to us.

But then, she was the one who took the first step of faith and asked. I had written off the luggage as lost for good.

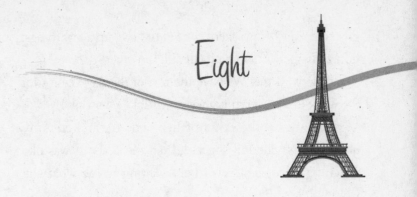

Eight

An hour later, after we each took a fabulous shower with a fragrant bar of hotel soap, and fluffy buttery croissants were resting merrily in our bellies, Amy gleefully wiggled into her skinny jeans. "They fit! I can zip them up easily. Look!"

"Voilá!" I said, sharing her moment of success. I poured myself another cup of coffee from a simple thermos coffeepot that was oh so elegantly French with its trim style.

"Travel agrees with me," Amy said in a brazen tone.

I laughed so hard I had to wipe the tears from my eyes. My friend had come a long way in twelve hours. Fresh starts like the one we were experiencing are so sweet after a disastrous first run. I had great hope that we were in for a much smoother ride from here on out.

"Would you mind if I unpacked everything before we

go exploring?" Amy asked. "I need to hang up a few things; hopefully the wrinkles will fall out."

"Fine with me. We have the rest of the day, the rest of the week to see everything we want. Take your time."

Settling on the edge of my bed, I watched Amy unpack. First one full suitcase, then the other. It was like watching a magic show; I kept waiting to see what she would pull out next.

"Do you have any white rabbits in there?"

"Any what?" She pulled out a long scarf, oblivious to how much she was mimicking an illusionist.

"I just can't believe how much you fit into those two suitcases."

I had hung up my four articles of interchangeable clothing in our narrow closet and had used two hangers. Amy used the other ten hotel hangers and then pulled out a dozen of her own metal ones. The next outfit she hung up was really something: a rich golden-colored sleeveless dress. It had a sash around the waist and a full skirt. The top was accented with shimmering brocade and came with a short jacket trimmed in the same extravagant material.

"Wow! Where did you get that? I've never seen that outfit."

"Grandmere made it when I was in college. I've never worn it."

"Amy, it's gorgeous." I stood up to examine the details.

"I know. And it fits me now. It was too small in college,

but I never told Grandmere after she sent it to me. Even when I couldn't wear it for the past twenty years, I just couldn't get rid of it."

"Hold it up. Oh, Amy, the color is beautiful with your hair and skin."

"I know it was crazy to pack this, but I thought I might wear it if we went out to some fancy place for dinner."

"Definitely." I glanced at my one wrinkle-free knee-length travel skirt and tried to think of what I'd wear if we actually did end up going somewhere nice enough for Amy to don her designer outfit.

"It's really beautiful," I said, focusing on Amy and not on my limited options. "And it's timeless, you know? It's the kind of outfit Grace Kelly could have worn in the fifties, yet it's still in style today."

Amy smiled. "Grandmere would have loved you even more for saying that."

Finishing the task of unpacking her excessive wardrobe, Amy reached for a final nibble of her neglected croissant and declared that she was ready to take on the day. We exited the hotel with a minimalist plan. We vaguely knew we wanted to start with the Musée d'Orsay, an art museum near our hotel. The Louvre seemed too daunting for our first day, and being less than eager to take another taxi or figure out the Metro system, we opted for a place close enough to walk.

As we stepped from under the protective and lengthy

portico arcade of the Rue de Rivoli and paused to cross the road, a zesty breeze caught up with us. We marched across a wide bridge marked "Pont Royal" and stopped halfway, buttoning up against the breeze.

"Let me take your picture." I motioned for Amy to stand by the railing. As I stepped back, Amy stretched out both arms as if wildly embracing the fresh air of Paris like a long-lost relative.

When I joined her by the side of the bridge, we paused to look down on the Seine River. The slow canal wound its way around the neck of medieval Paris like a green ruffled boa. The ancient face of this city was certainly age-creviced beyond anything a vat of wrinkle cream could do for her. But she was regal and proud and greeted us with her shoulders back and her chin forward.

We crossed the bridge and stood in line for tickets to the Musée d'Orsay, which was located in the huge trans-formed central train station. I skimmed the tour book, trying to remember why Amy wanted to come here first. The book said the Orsay museum was proud host to art from the 1800s, which meant it was rich in examples of impressionism. This was the place to experience the best of the works of artists such as Renoir, Degas, Cézanne, van Gogh, Gauguin, Manet, and, of course, Monet.

Amy's reasons for coming here were clear. These were all her favorites. We picked up a brochure in English and made our way past a maze of bold statues. Amy headed for the elevator up to the impressionist level, where she entered her garden of delight and buzzed from one work of art to another like an overachieving bumblebee.

"Ooh, look! *Water Lilies* by Monet!" Amy was beaming.

We stood next to a woman with honey golden hair who was calmly observing the painting Amy was so excited to see. It was a familiar pastel blue painting of a footbridge over a tranquil lily pond.

"Would you like to know a little piece of trivia?" The woman smiled warmly.

"Sure," Amy said.

"Monet actually built the bridge you see in all these paintings. He designed it based on an engraving he had of a Japanese bridge. The bridge and his home are located about an hour from here in Giverny."

"Really?" I was drawn in now.

The woman nodded, warming up to the topic. "Monet painted *en plein air*. Outside. He learned this from Boudin. Monet often rose at 5:00 a.m. and wandered along the river in Giverny observing the rows of poplars and the fields of red poppies."

"That explains why he kept painting poplars and water lilies," Amy added.

"Yes and no. Monet said he wanted to reproduce what existed between the subject and himself. He wanted to capture the elusive feel of light, sound, and air and express those qualities in his artwork. Do you see? He painted the same subjects over and over but captured them at different times of day and under different conditions to give the sense of what was happening in that untouchable space between the artist and the subject."

"What brochure did you pick up at the door?" Amy fanned the thin flyer we were handed when we paid for our admission. "I'd like to get the one you have."

"No brochure." The woman blushed. "I'm sorry if I went on too much."

"No," we both said.

"That was fascinating. Do you work here?" I asked.

"No. I lead art tours, though. My group left yesterday. I don't go home until tonight, so I thought I'd slip in for one more afternoon of gazing. I'm Jill, by the way."

"I'm Amy. This is Lisa. We're from Lexington. How about you?"

"Wellington."

"Where is Wellington?" I asked.

"Oh, sorry. Wellington, New Zealand. I forget that my American accent throws people off. I grew up in California, but now I live in New Zealand."

For the next hour and a half Amy and I sank ourselves gratefully into the most amazing private art tour with Jill. We learned that Monet had astigmatism as well as cataracts and painted the world as he literally saw it with all the colors blurred. We studied van Gogh's bedroom and his self-portrait that he painted three months before committing suicide. Jill encouraged us to linger over a glass display case that held a statue of a ballerina by Degas. The statue posed for us with her chin up and best pointed toe forward.

"Look at the details. The illusion of depth and the even muscle tone," Jill said. "Now look at the face. Do you feel the personality of the young woman who modeled for this piece?"

I was so grateful for the way Jill opened our eyes to details Amy and I would have flitted right past. All these great pieces held so much character and story.

We entered another room and Amy said, "Ooh, my grandmere had a copy of this painting in her bedroom. I never realized it was a Renoir."

Jill told us the background of the familiar outdoor scene in which a crowd of women and men in Victorian garb were dancing and dining. The painting *Ball at the Moulin de la Galette, Montmartre* had been painted in 1876.

"There is so much life and movement in the art from this period," Amy said. "It amazes me how many of these pieces were painted right here, in and around Paris."

Jill smiled a knowing smile at us, her compliant pupils. "That's why I always bring my groups here first, before I take them to the Louvre."

"Well!" Amy nodded to me. "I'm glad to know we made one wise decision so far. We arrived last night, and our introduction to Paris was a little bumpy."

"Oh?" Jill looked at us sympathetically.

"It's a long story," I said. "If you have time to hear it, I think we should at least treat you to lunch to thank you for the private tour."

"I've already eaten, but a cup of tea would be nice," Jill said.

"We heard that Angelina's is good. It's on the same street as our hotel, so we know it's not far," Amy suggested.

"Of course the recommendation for Angelina's came from the taxi driver who stole our luggage," I added as we headed out the door.

"Stole your luggage?" Now Jill was the eager listener.

We retraced our steps toward our hotel and filled her in on the escapades of our first night in Paris.

"Unbelievable," she said as we crossed the Pont Royal again and glanced at the tour boats meandering their way up the river. "And you two haven't even been here twenty-four hours."

"I know. Frightening, isn't it?" I said.

We all laughed, and Jill added, "I'd say you're definitely having a Sisterchicks adventure."

"Sisterchicks." Amy turned to me. "What a great word! Best friends but with a little attitude going on. I like that. That's us, Lisa. We're Sisterchicks."

We started walking again, and Amy grabbed my arm. She pretended to throw me over the bridge and into the river.

"What are you doing?" I squawked.

"Sisterchicks go in Seine!" she spouted. "Get it? Go insane? Go in Seine?"

Jill's highly contagious laughter filled the *plein air* around us, prompting Amy and me to laugh with her.

The buoyant camaraderie continued at a lively pace. We came upon a charming sedate café, and Jill said, "Would you mind if we stopped here instead of Angelina's? I need to use the restroom. I've been here before. It's very nice."

"We don't mind," Amy said, and I nodded my agreement.

We entered the intimate little café filled with Parisians. Amy and Jill both went off to find the restroom while I waited for them by the front counter. I was asked something several times. I assumed I was being asked if I wanted to be seated. I shook my head, said thank you in French, and tried to look like I knew what I was doing.

Beside me on the counter I noticed two plates with small pieces of cut-up pastries. One looked like a cream-filled éclair. The other pastry I didn't recognize. Assuming them to be free samples, I took a bite of each. The éclair was especially good; I reached for another small piece.

That's when I noticed people were looking at me. I'm not paranoid by nature, and I really was trying to overcome my biased opinions of Paris. But these people were staring at me. They were talking about me, too. I just didn't know what they were saying. I wondered if this was a locals-only sort of place, and they realized I was an out-sider.

I considered finding a table instead of standing here, so obviously American and lost. But I didn't see any empty spaces. Reaching for another sample of the éclair, I checked the corners of my mouth to make sure I didn't have big globs of chocolate stuck to my face.

A man in a suit stepped up and spoke to me in French. He placed a plate with a knife and half of a croissant next to the other samples on the counter.

I smiled.

He pointed at the sign above the counter, which was, of course, in French. Then he pointed at the plate he had just placed next to the other samples. He seemed to be waiting for me to say or do something.

I assumed he was adding to the selection of samples so I said, "Merci," picked up the knife, and demurely cut off a corner of the croissant.

The man went ballistic. He waved his hands in my face and pointed to the door.

I scurried outside, my heart pounding as I waited for Amy and Jill to find me.

"There you are." Amy stepped out of the restaurant a few achingly long moments later. "What are you doing out here?"

"I think it's a locals-only place. The manager made me leave."

"Why would he do that?" Jill asked. "I've eaten here before."

"I don't know. I was standing there waiting, and this man in a suit came up and pointed to a sign on the counter and then yelled at me."

"What did the sign say?" Jill asked.

"I have no idea."

"I'll go find out," Amy slipped back inside and returned shaking her head. "I don't understand what the problem was."

"What did the sign say?" I asked.

Amy gave a shrug and repeated the posted message word for word. "Please place your dirty plates here."

Nine

I scurried away from the café window as fast as I could, with Jill and Amy hot on my heels. They pelted me with questions for half a block. I stopped in front of a pet store window and blurted out what had happened, how I had stood there in front of all those sophisticated Parisians "sampling" everyone's leftovers from their dirty dishes.

Amy pressed her lips together. Her eyes were huge, but she didn't uncork her reaction until she was sure I'd be okay with it. She looked at Jill and back at me. Jill was turning red in the face and didn't appear to be breathing.

Realizing that the two of them might pass out in front of me due to their extremely good manners, I let loose with the laughter bomb, shattering the decorum I'd already lost. We laughed until we cried, clinging to each other and leaning against the storefront window so we wouldn't fall over in hysterics. A man from inside the pet store came out and shooed us down the street, away from his customers.

We laughed all the way to the entrance of Angelina's. This time all three of us had to use the restroom after laughing so much. Amy insisted I go with her and Jill so they could keep an eye on me.

We calmed ourselves and took our seats by the front window where we ordered chocolate drinks and joined in a toast. The goblet-sized specialty drinks arrived at our table wearing thick dollops of whipped cream on top like a French boudoir wig from the court of Louis XIV.

With white moustaches all around, we laughed some more in this larger, airier café. A well-dressed grandmere and a young boy in a school uniform with an embroidered patch on his blazer pocket sat together. As he dipped his long spoon into his dish of ice cream, he seemed to be telling her a story that made her smile. At another table a man sat reading a newspaper while the woman across from him was pressing buttons on her cell phone. No one in this friendly café seemed to notice that the three of us weren't laughing in French.

I loved listening to Jill laugh. Her wonderful giggle took the sting out of my grand faux pas.

We settled into a chatty sort of conversation by the time we were drinking ourselves down to the layer of chocolate moustaches. Jill told us this was her fourth trip to Paris. Leading art tours was a midlife sort of dream that her best friend, Kathy, had talked her into pursuing.

"It's been wonderful," she said. "I haven't had any significant problems during the past three trips."

"Well, then you might not want to hang around us too much," Amy said. "We do seem to attract more than our share of 'special moments,' as my mother-in-law would call them. We're not like this at home. Really."

"You will forgive me, won't you, if I have a hard time believing that," Jill said.

"I guess we do have our moments at home, too, but it's all been a little more compact and intense since we left," Amy said. "If we didn't have the assurance that God was taking care of us every step of the way, I'm sure we'd both be a mess by now."

Jill smiled and nodded.

I knew then that the three of us had more in common than a bunch of giggles.

"It's His mercies, you know," Jill said. "They really are new every morning."

"Yes, they are," Amy agreed.

I didn't want any of this to end. The sound of Jill's laughter. The way the waning sunlight was coming through the front window of Angelina's and touching off firefly sparks from Amy's jewelry every time she turned her head. Each glittery bead in her necklace seemed to have its own spark of life. All of them were dancing around her neck like a Renoir painting packed with vibrant Victorians picnicking on a summer afternoon.

Every woman of every generation deserved to sit in the sunlight with such friends on such an afternoon and laugh and sip chocolate and know in her heart that God's mercy would be new again the next morning.

Jill's art lessons had gone inside me. My eyes had been opened to impressionism. These things around me were familiar: Amy, chocolate, tables, chairs. But something was different. Ethereal. Something mysterious was at work in the space between my surroundings and me. A sort of translucent beauty that was hidden in that untouchable space where there are no maverick molecules.

How does a human capture that sort of nearly invisible motion and magnificence?

My heart beat a strange rhythm. It was as if something eternal had passed over my thoughts. I almost glimpsed something beyond comprehension. But what? It came so close my spirit reached with all five fingers of my senses, longing to touch whatever it was.

Was that You, God?

I wanted to run after Him. Him! God. Amy's Papa. My almighty, omnipotent, heavenly Father who was untouchable and unfathomable.

He passed by, and my heart surged at the possibility.

A clear thought settled on me. God was the artist. Every molecule was set in obedient motion to Him in this space between Himself and His subject. That space swirled with calculated mystery. Yet I, the subject of His affection, was the maverick. Ever resisting.

"Ready, Lisa?"

"I'm sorry. What?"

"Jill just said she has to get going to make her flight. Do you want to leave, too, or stay a little longer?"

"We can go. Sorry. I just got a little spacey there for a minute."

"Ah, the joys of jet lag," Jill said. "Try to take lots of vitamin C. And sleep, of course, when you can."

We exchanged our contact information, and before Jill caught a taxi at the curb, she hugged us both warmly and invited us to visit her any time in Wellington. We returned the invitation, but somehow going to Kentucky didn't sound quite as exciting as New Zealand.

"Are you okay?" Amy asked as we walked the short distance back to our hotel.

I nodded. "Just thinking. Taking it all in."

"Do you want to see something else now? Or should we go back to our room and call it a day?"

"It's such a calm evening, after the wind this afternoon. What about taking a boat ride?"

"I'm in," Amy said.

"Let's hope you're not all the way in," I said.

She didn't catch my attempt to compete with her earlier joke, so I explained it to her. "You're in, but not all the way in because if you were all the way in, that would make you in Seine."

Apparently her earlier pun now escaped her, and she looked confused.

"Never mind." I remembered how my dad used to say that if you had to explain a joke, it wasn't really a joke, and therefore it didn't bear repeating.

Retracing our steps to the Pont Royal, Amy and I walked down the steps to the river level and bought two tickets for a ride in a covered passenger boat. The bench seat we selected near the front accommodated the two of us with room to spare. Only a few others joined us for our evening cruise. By the way they were dressed, several of the passengers looked as if they were commuting or on their way to meet someone for dinner. This certainly was a leisurely way to go.

"It looks different from this level, doesn't it?" Amy said.

"What looks different?"

"Paris. The city. The buildings. You have to look up to see anything, and none of it appears the same as it did when we were viewing it from our hotel window."

"You know, I read in one of the guide books that if you want to get a unique view of Paris, you can take a tour of the sewers."

"You can't be serious," Amy said. "That's not my idea of a good time."

"Mine either."

"I like this speed." Amy leaned back and gazed out the glass top of the boat to view the bridge we were motoring under. "I want to see as much as we can of Paris. Just not from the heights or the depths."

"Heights?"

"I don't do heights. You know that."

I tried to remember if I knew that Amy had a thing about heights. It had been years since she and I had done anything that required significant elevation. She hadn't expressed any fear when we boarded the plane or when she looked out the hotel room window.

Her next sentence began with, "Ever since your brother Will…" and then a distinct memory returned to me.

Amy and I were nine or ten years old. We were playing outside at my house when Amy threw my brother's football onto the roof. The football got stuck at the edge along the gutter. Will brought out a ladder, and then he made Amy climb up it to retrieve the football. She accepted the task, but then my brother shook the ladder and teased her.

I yelled at him to stop. Amy froze and clung to the rungs, unable to move up or down. After I threatened to tell on him, Will finally stopped shaking the ladder. It still took a lot of coaxing before Amy tapped the football loose, and it tumbled to the ground.

Hanging on for dear life, she called down something that made Will crack up. "Gravity always works, doesn't it?"

I knew she was afraid. But it did seem odd for her to

be thinking of scientific principles at such a moment.

"Come on, Isaac Newton," Will called up to her. "I have to put away the ladder." Then he gave the ladder another shake.

I screamed at him and told him to bug off.

Poor Amy couldn't move. She stayed on that ladder, clinging to the rungs for a long time before I could make my annoying brother go away. Once he left with his heckling laughter, I talked Amy down one rung at a time. She crumpled to the ground, patting the earth like a lost pet that had returned. I'd never seen her so shaken.

"Lisa," she had said with a quivering voice, "promise me you'll never make me climb up a ladder again for the rest of my life."

I promised her I wouldn't, and as far as I knew, she never had climbed a ladder again.

That memory made me realize something I suppose I knew from the beginning of our friendship: Amy needed to know she could trust people. That's why she continually extracted promises from me during our childhood. She was testing my loyalty. My devotion must have no longer been in question because she hadn't asked me to promise her anything for years.

I had a feeling that might change before this trip was over.

Our boat slowed as it approached the landing near the Eiffel Tower. The evening had pacified itself with a soft blanket of twilight. Amber flecks of sunlight seemed to evaporate from the sky dot by dot. They transferred their glow to dozens of lights in the city that rose above us.

As we left the boat and climbed the steps, we saw where the dots of broken sun had gone. Streetlights, car lights, lights in cafés, and lights in apartment windows all began to come on one by one. The City of Lights was warming up. Soon she would show us her symphony of brilliance.

We stood together at street level, speechless. Before us stood the magnificent icon of Paris. *La Tour Eiffel*. The enormous structure rose from the earth with a grandeur that confused the senses.

At first approach, the Eiffel Tower seemed of such mountainous proportions that it appeared to have sprouted from the earth on its own. It was like a fixture that had always been there, like the Seine. At the same time, the monstrosity looked so see-through and fragile that one gale-force wind would be all that was needed to blow the whole thing down like a child's tower of toothpicks. I remembered feeling the same overwhelming sense of complexities the first time I walked underneath the Eiffel Tower more than two decades ago.

"You know the Eiffel Tower shouldn't still be here," I said. "It was set up for a world's fair and was supposed to be taken down afterward, but they bolstered it up, and it's still here."

"And exactly when was it supposed to be demolished?" Amy asked.

"I don't remember. The late 1800s, I think."

Amy had redirected her attention to a Parisian vendor who sported a white chef's hat and coat. He stood inside a small trailer holding a shallow frying pan and working over a small set of burners. A wonderful fragrance wafted our way.

"What does that smell like to you? Waffle cones?" I asked.

"Or crepes." Amy sniffed the air with a more developed sensitivity for French food. "Ooh, doesn't a crepe sound delicious right now?"

"Crêpe suzette," I said, reading the sign that came into view over the trailer as Amy and I approached. A line had formed, and we soon knew why. This chef delivered a puppet show along with his gourmet crepes-to-go. His right hand was covered with a thick oven mitt that was shaped like an alligator. The alligator gripped the long handle of the frying pan and randomly would pop up and have a look at the crowd with googly eyes on top of its head.

Two small children who stood to the side with their watchful parents called out to the alligator. The alligator was busy shaking the pan and not responding. They called out again and giggled. I had no idea what language they were speaking.

The alligator suddenly seemed to notice them and

lunged forward with a snap. They were thrilled. And so were the rest of us. The entire time the chef was at work, he didn't appear to look up at the customers or interact with them. Mr. Alligator handled all his public relations.

Amy and I stepped to the front of the line, and the alligator asked in French what we wanted. I poked Amy and told her in a whisper to order for me. The alligator was staring at me, and I didn't want to get snapped at. Amy chose something from the list of five options on the menu posted on the side of the trailer. She paid the woman who was sitting in a covert corner inside the trailer, balancing the cash box on her lap.

Two crepes were prepared efficiently in two separate pans, but with alligator's watchful attention to each as they cooked simultaneously. One of the crepes simmered with a mixture of ham, cheese, and shallots. The other one was stuffed with sliced strawberries, drizzled with chocolate sauce, and dolloped with a dab of whipping cream. With his un-puppeted hand, the chef flipped the thin pancake into the shape of what looked to me like a neatly folded burrito.

Receiving our tidy treats, we both offered a "merci" to the glaring alligator that seemed to watch us walk away. We found an open bench and shared our dinner, in *plein air*, lounging in the shadow of the Eiffel Tower.

Suddenly the four-legged giant before us lit up. The lights ran up all four sides at the same moment and pulsated several times, like a strobe light.

"Come on." I urged Amy to take the last bite. "Let's cross the street and take a closer look."

Amy seemed to hang back as I boldly approached the great edifice. I grinned at her over my shoulder. "It's not going to bite you."

"I know." Amy picked up her pace and arrived at the underbelly of the creature three full steps before me. She looked up at the optical illusion of so many "sticks" holding the tower in place.

I pulled out my camera and took a picture of Amy looking up with her mouth open. Then I took a picture of the internal inversion. I doubted the shot would come out, even with the flash, because it was so dark.

"We're going to come back later to take pictures of us in front," I said.

"Take a picture of me over here." Amy wove her way through the throng of tourists milling around, and I followed. I found it amazing to be around so many people and to hear different languages. Some of the tourists stood in line to buy tickets for one of the elevators that would take them to the top. Others came down from their ride to one of the three levels and talked with their friends. Their gestures were animated, and their expressions were flushed.

Amy reached one of the four "legs" of the Eiffel Tower and put both her hands on the huge metal support. "Here. Take my picture." She leaned so it looked as if she were single-handedly holding up the column.

I made sure the flash was on as she warmed up to the beast. "Beauty and the Beast!" I called out as I snapped the picture. Amy didn't catch the connection, but that was okay. She was slowly making friends with the Eiffel Tower, and I knew that was going to be an important first step before she would be willing to step into one of the compact elevators and take the ride of her life to the top.

I just hoped she didn't view the triangle-shaped structure as the world's largest ladder, because from up at the top, there would be no doubt that gravity worked. All the time.

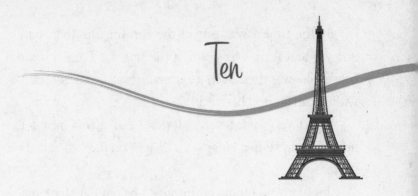

Ten

We didn't go up the Eiffel Tower that second night in Paris. I didn't even bring it up as an option. We had time. I knew Amy would want to come back.

The next morning she was up before I was. I woke when I heard her singing in the shower. Joel was a morning person, too. It never ceased to amaze me how chipper morning people could be. It wasn't natural.

Rolling over and reaching for the phone, I called room service. Fortunately, the hotel employee taking calls was willing to answer me in English and even asked if I wanted cream with the coffee.

"I ordered an omelet," I told Amy when she emerged with a towel wrapped around her wet hair. "And coffee."

"Oh, good. I was just thinking I could go for an omelet this morning. Thanks, Lisa."

By the time I was out of the shower, the food had arrived, and Amy was pouring the fragrant French roast coffee. She was dressed in a skirt and sweater accessorized with a scarf around her neck.

"Don't you look lovely?" I wondered if this meant I needed to dress up a bit as well. "What's on the tour schedule for today?"

"It's sunny, so I thought this might be our day to hit the Champs-Elysées. We could walk there, through the park. What do you think?"

Clearly, this was Amy's D-day in France. Forget the World War II landing on the beaches of Normandy. Today was "Debutante Day," and Amy was ready!

I tried to select a "fancy" outfit to wear, but I wasn't a fancy sort of dresser. What I had brought with me was practical and not very exciting. Nevertheless, I was out the door with Amy before ten o'clock and armed with all my spending money. The stores wouldn't know what hit them!

Strolling the length of the covered arcade of the Rue de Rivoli, Amy and I took our time, window shopping but not buying anything yet. It didn't make sense to us to buy something that was down the way from our hotel and then carry it with us for the rest of the day.

Amy spotted a designer shop, and we took a detour down a side street that opened up into another wide boulevard lined with impressive, classy old buildings. We ended up passing the Ritz Hotel, and that's when we knew we were out of our element. The first shop we went into was a clothing store that carried a designer label I wasn't familiar with. Amy took one quick look around, and we exited with a polite "*au revoir*" to the shop attendant who looked at us with disdain.

"This was not what I had in mind when I thought we could do some shopping," Amy said once we were outside the exclusive shop. "Let's find some stores where we can afford to buy something."

We headed back the way we had entered the high-end area and came out at the Place de la Concorde. I pulled out the map to get our bearings. To our left was the main section of the Tuileries Gardens that we had viewed from our hotel window. That portion of the gardens covered well over a mile and seemed to roll itself out from the Louvre's courtyard. A note on the map said that the far-reaching gardens were begun in the 1600s and showed meticulous attention to symmetry. It was the Central Park of Paris with rows of shady trees, gravel walkways, ponds for floating toy sailboats, open-air cafés, and elaborate fountains. The park came to an abrupt halt at a wide intersection where we now stood. In front of us zoomed a steady flow of traffic.

"Look." Amy pointed to the front of a gated compound to our right. "It's the American Embassy."

"That's always good to know," I said with a nod to the two uniformed marines who stood at the entrance.

"Do you have any idea what that is?" Amy motioned to a pointed obelisk in the center of the traffic circle that punctuated the air like an exclamation mark. In front of it was a huge fountain with an imposing statue.

"I have no idea." I looked around to get a point of reference from the landmarks and to make sure I was reading the map correctly. "If that's the Fleur de Lis Hotel behind us, then this is the Place de la Concorde."

"That's the Fleur de Lis Hotel?" Amy spun around. "You're kidding! Grandmere talked about that hotel. She went there one time when she was young. For tea. She said she wore gloves and had to sit up straight the whole time. We should go there, Lisa. For tea. Just like Grandmere did."

"Sounds good to me. Do you still want to know about this seventy-two-foot obelisk here at the Place de la Concorde?"

"Sure."

"The book says it's a 2,300-year-old-relic and was a gift to Paris in the early 1800s from Egypt." I read the final line from the guidebook. "'A plaque in front of the obelisk marks the location where the guillotine was used during the French Revolution to remove over two thousand citizens from their heads.'"

Amy and I looked at each other with a matching expression of discomfort. Neither of us was prepared for this gruesome bit of French history. Especially when the small detail of the loss of two thousand lives was delivered with a poor attempt at humor.

Amy looked at the book and finished the last paragraph for me. "'Marie Antoinette was among the thousands who met with the guillotine's blade on this square.'"

We looked at each other in solemn remembrance as the swirl of vehicles made their whiplash turns around the fountain and obelisk, heading for the bridge across the Seine.

"Do you know much about the French Revolution?" Amy asked.

"No. All I remember was that the peasants went crazy and stormed the Bastille prison to set the prisoners free."

"I know that was the start," Amy said. "But once the royalty had been removed from the throne, no one trusted anyone to make decisions and run the new republic. Grandmere used to say the birth of liberty in France was a bloody birth. Too many innocents were wrongly accused and beheaded along with the rebels."

"So many lives lost." I glanced at the tour book. A side note caught my eye. "Wow," I said under my breath.

"What?"

"It says the bridge underpass where Princess Diana lost her life is three bridges downstream from here at Pont de l'Alma."

"Wasn't she coming from the Ritz Hotel that night? We just walked past that hotel."

"I know."

We stood together looking at the map in the tour book. All around us rushed the city's noise. Diesel fumes floated our way from a large truck that aggressively took the turn. We were within walking distance of original art that had filled our imaginations yesterday with freedom and life. Yet at the same time we were within walking distance of where two princesses had died a hundred and fifty years apart from each other.

"This city," Amy said in a low rumble. "It's not what I expected."

"I know." I didn't tell Amy what I think she already knew. Paris was the city I loved to hate.

"This way." Amy pointed toward the second part of the Tuileries that led to the Champs-Elysées. Along the path ahead of us a dozen varieties of flowering trees were in their final bloom, tossing the last of their pink and white confetti in the air. Spring had thrown her once-a-year party, and we were the latecomers. Our shoes were the bristles, our legs the broomsticks clearing away the evidence of a good time that was had by all.

A single red-tipped bird swooped in front of us on the wide path, twittering his apology for nearly bumping into us. The enamored fellow obviously had been one of the revelers at the spring party. That explained why he was still a little loopy.

Amy and I fell into step, subconsciously matching our

strides the same way we had when we were young and walked home from school every day to my house. I believe a calm contentment comes to a woman's heart, even in the midst of newness, when she is accompanied by one sweet familiarity. Today that familiarity was the gait of my dearest friend.

We were still us.

It didn't matter how old we were or what we weighed or what color our hair was at that moment. No one had to tell us how to fall in stride. We knew how to do that.

"Amy?"

"Yeah?"

"Thanks for bringing me to Paris with you."

She smiled. "I was just going to thank you for coming with me."

"This is really a dream for you—for us—isn't it? I was trying to remember how old we were when you first gave me visions of sauntering through these gardens and down the Champs-Elysées like we were a couple of refined women of influence."

Amy lifted her chin a little higher. "The way I see it, you and I have become so chic in our maturing years that we don't need a fluffy poodle on the end of a pink leather leash to make our grand entrance promenading down the Champs-Elysées."

"That's a good thing since neither of us happened to bring a poodle."

"We are a couple of classy women who are full of style just beggin' to be shown off on this street of all streets."

I laughed and added my well-wishes for our dream-come-true moment. "Well, in that case, ooh la la, baby. Champs-Elysées, look out! Here we come!"

The grand boulevard of Paris was alive with shoppers and visitors from all corners of the globe. As we waited at a traffic light with a throng of humanity in all shapes, sizes, and skin tones, I wondered if any of them had grown up with the same illusion as Amy. Did they imagine they had "arrived" as well?

When the light changed, we strode the wide width of the intersection and paraded down the tree-lined sidewalk with our heads twisting right and then left to take in everything.

"Ooh, Sephora!" Amy pointed to a perfume shop. "We have to go there."

I blithely followed Amy into the huge cavern of a store. The palace of fragrance was decorated in granite and chrome. Guards dressed in all black and wearing communication wires in their ears stood at the entrance and throughout the store. The side walls were lined with glass cases, and inside the cases were hundreds of glass presentation pedestals, each holding an ornate bottle of perfume.

Heavy-handed techno music beat like jungle drums, driving us deeper into the fragrance jungle where instincts took over, and we began sniffing at every sample bottle we saw on display.

"I don't know about you," Amy said, "but I'm not leaving here until I find some perfume to take home with me."

Amy's declaration infused our hunt for the perfect new fragrance with a frenzied vitality. We started to try on every perfume, the same way we had when we were thirteen and Amy's neighbor Mrs. Roberts invited us to see her brand new Avon home-tester case. Poor Mrs. Roberts. Every one of her samples was thoroughly tested by Amy and me. I'm sure Mrs. Roberts hoped to acquire some of our hard-earned babysitting money. But in the end, we didn't buy anything. Amy and I came home with four tiny lipstick samples that were an inch big and smelled like crayon wax. Amy's mother decreed that our forearms smelled like a fruit ambrosia salad that needed to go back in the fridge.

"It's so hard to decide." Amy stood by a display of perfumes that all bore names in French. She sniffed one wrist and then the other.

I'd stopped using my available skin as the testing ground and had dabbed fragrances onto the small tester papers provided. I fanned out the dozen white strips in my hand. "Pick a perfume. Any perfume."

"This one." Amy randomly pulled one out of the middle.

I sprayed my wrist with that fragrance, sniffed it again, and sneezed.

A beautiful young saleswoman dressed in all black, with midnight black hair and ivory skin, stepped over with a shaker of coffee beans and a tissue. She handed me the tissue and then told us to breathe in the strong scent of the coffee beans to clear our sense of smell.

"Much better," I said. "Thanks."

She asked if we needed any direction.

"This may be a silly question, but do you carry Chanel perfumes?" Amy asked.

"Of course. Thees way, s'il vous plaît."

We followed, and Amy picked up one of the sample bottles. She closed her eyes and gave a tiny spritz of the familiar fragrance. Then, as if remembering a pleasant dream, she said, "My grandmere just walked into the room. This is what she wore for years. I have to buy some. Is this your smallest bottle?"

"Oui."

"Excuse me." A woman with a British accent smiled at the assistant. "Would you please direct me to some fragrances that have light floral tones but don't include jasmine as one of the ingredients?"

"Certainly. Thees way."

"Do you mind if we tag along?" I asked, about to sneeze again. "It sounds like you and I are looking for the same sort of perfume."

The woman gave us a broad smile and nod, as we fell in line like Sneezy, Sleepy, and Happy behind our very own

Snow White. We were off to mine the gems of this fragrance cavern.

"By chance did either of you go to the perfume workshop offered by the Bon Voyage Tour Company?" Happy asked us.

"No," I said.

"I had the pleasure two days ago. That's how I knew what to ask for. The workshop is three hours; you have to reserve ahead of time. You smell samples and learn how perfume is made. It was very interesting. Fairly expensive, but I'm glad I went."

Our Snow White apparently wasn't about to be outdone by a workshop offered by one of the local perfumeries. She gathered us close at one of the impeccable displays and with her lovely French accent described how a single perfume "note" could be comprised of a combination of five hundred ingredients. She explained the way the "top notes" dance off the skin almost immediately.

"Think of zee middle notes as the heart of the fragrance that sets zee tone. Zee base notes give depth and last for days and sometimes for years."

Amy and I shared a nod of agreement. Those few liquid granules of Amy's grandmere's fragrance still lingered and reminded us both of her.

"It's like buying a bottle of memories," Amy murmured.

After more direction on warm tones, cool tones, floral

tones, and earth tones, Happy made her selection and left us to go to the cash register.

Amy and I lingered as Snow White lowered her chin and took us into her confidence. "Fragrance presents a person to zee world. When Marie Antoinette came through zee streets of Paris, it is said zee people knew it was she by zee scent coming from her carriage. Napoleon carried a flask of cologne always in his boot. His scent was of lemon, rosemary, and rich sandalwood."

Mesmerized by her passion for fragrance, Amy and I willingly reached for bottles of perfume that we knew had to come home with us. I bought the smallest bottle and knew at the price I was paying I would use it sparingly. Amy went a little crazy and bought three bottles. One was for her mom. Our lovely Snow White included extra free samples of perfume and lotion in our elegant shopping bags and waved to us as we left.

Spectacularly fragrant and culturally enriched, Amy and I sashayed our way down the Champs-Elysées with smiles on our contented faces. We held the handles of our shopping bags as daintily as if we were holding pink leashes to prancing poodles.

Ooh la la! We were classy, sassy, and just looking for chocolate.

"What do you think, Lisa? Should we stop at a café and watch the world go by?"

A twinge of past Parisian memories clenched my stomach and raced up to my throat, choking the goldenness of our chic moment.

"How about that café?" Amy asked. "Why don't we go there?"

"No!" I squawked. "Not that one."

Amy stopped to study my expression.

"We need to go to the Ladurée," I said, in a moment of quick thinking. "Did I tell you about Ladurée? It's a Victorian teahouse just down the way. Very pink and fun. You'll love it."

"Okay. Do you remember where it is?"

"No, not exactly."

Amy pulled out the map, found Ladurée with ease, and led the way with a cloud of sweet, complex fragrance still following her. I was the cloud. A very wisteria-and-lavender sort of cloud.

We entered Ladurée and were led upstairs to the grand salon and into a room that was about as pink as I had remembered it to be. Seating ourselves on a pink-tufted bench seat by the window, we were only inches away from the guests at the adjoining table. I'd forgotten how dining space was different in European restaurants. At first Amy kept glancing over at the expressive man next to us talking in low tones to the woman across the small table from him. I wondered if Amy would be too uncomfortable with this setup, especially since she could more than likely under-stand everything they were saying.

We held up the menus and whispered between the two of us as if we, too, had important matters to discuss. Soon enough, we both settled in and accepted the close quarters.

"How come I feel like I'm back in my childhood bedroom?" Amy asked.

"It's the pink. And the ruffles. Was I right? Do you love this?"

"Yes. *Très élégante!*"

Our decisions were easy. A piece of chocolate cake to split and two macaroons. We also ordered pots of tea.

"So." Amy folded her hands and leaned across the table. "I have something to ask you."

"Okay."

She tilted her head. Amy knew me far too well for my own good. "Lisa, when are you going to tell me?"

Eleven

"Tell you what?" I asked nonchalantly, stirring a pinch more sugar into my Darjeeling tea.

"Your Paris story," Amy said without glancing at the other diners in the Victorian teahouse. "When are you going to tell me the whole story? I want to hear what happened to you here twenty years ago. I know something did."

I could feel my heart rate picking up but tried to keep my expression static so she wouldn't notice the tears in my eyes. All they needed to do was push the first one over the edge, and the rest would follow. I didn't want to start the cascade here or now—not with strangers sitting a few inches away. Especially after I had done such a stellar job the past few days of ignoring all the memories I had of this city and the paralyzing feelings that always accompanied those memories.

"Ask me later," I said. "I can't tell you now."

This was another one of Amy's shining moments. She always honored my boundaries, never questioning or pushing. Not when it came to my mother's rule about Barbies and not now. Amy always said, "okay" and never made me feel I owed her something in return for her kind favor.

The thing I realized after we began to sip our imported loose-leaf tea was that she knew. I'd never told her any details about Paris or my broken heart. Joel didn't know. My brothers didn't know. My mother, of course, didn't know. I hadn't told anyone. But Amy knew. She knew about Gerard, even though I had never mentioned his name.

I suppose an individual couldn't walk in stride with you for so many years and not notice even the tiniest hitch in your step when a pebble sneaks into your shoe. Gerard was the pebble in the corner of my heart that would not fall out no matter how many times I'd tried to shake out the memories.

I realized that by answering with not now, I was finally admitting to Amy and to myself that I did have a story to tell. Up until that moment I had managed to convince myself there was nothing to tell. But now I even invited her to ask me later.

I'm sure the chocolate was divine. The macaroons are one of Ladurée's specialties, but I couldn't tell what they tasted like. I listened to Amy and smiled. I took appreciative bites and dabbed the chocolate from my lips. But none of it filled me. What I was really doing was sobbing on the inside. The tears found my resolve too strong, and so they retreated, cascading back into the corner of my heart they had kept flooded all these years.

We split our bill, bought some more goodies at the bakery counter downstairs, and ventured back out to the sweet afternoon air.

Our next tentatively scheduled event was to go the rest of the distance on the Champs-Elysées and see the Arch of Triumph.

We approached the grand memorial and stood at a distance, just as we had with the Eiffel Tower. Amy held the tour book and read the details about how Napoleon had commissioned the construction of this impressive archway to celebrate another victory after one of his many battles.

I stood back, fighting one of my own battles. The top observation deck of the Arch of Triumph held a few too many memories for me. From up there, I had once looked out over all of Paris and marveled at the way the tree-lined boulevards stretched out like spokes from that central hub. All the lines of my young adult life seemed to start at the same point and radiate out to points unknown.

I had felt as if I were on top of the world as Gerard's arms enveloped me. All of the future for me, for the two of us, stretched out from that place and from that moment with possibilities as endless as Paris's charm. I was so naïve. So vulnerable. So willing to believe that anything could happen. A suave, twenty-seven-year-old Frenchman really could be in love with me. It was not too far-fetched to believe that he would wait for me. I felt free that day. I was happy. Fully accessorized with glittering hope.

"Do you want to go up to the top?" Amy broke into my thoughts.

"No," I said quickly. "Do you?"

She shook her head. "The tour book says you have to climb a network of narrow spiral steps. I don't think I can do that."

"Are you sure? It is the Arch of Triumph, you know."

"I know."

I wasn't sure why I was trying to convince Amy to go up, except that she didn't have memories of this place yet. I didn't want to hold her back. "The view is amazing. You can see all over Paris. You might be sorry later if you don't go up to the top."

She hesitated before saying, "I'm going to pass. If I'm sorry later, I'll just have to live with being sorry. I don't mind waiting, if you want to go up without me."

"No, that's okay. I've already seen the view from the top. It's an experience I don't need to repeat."

"We have lots of other things to see," Amy said.

"There's Montmartre, Notre Dame, the Louvre."

"Not to mention the visit we need to make to the family Grandmere wanted you to see."

Amy nodded.

"Are you avoiding that visit?" I asked.

"I don't think I'm avoiding it exactly. I'm nervous about my French being good enough to communicate."

"Amy, you've been communicating fantastically with everyone since we arrived. There's nothing wrong with your French. If you didn't speak and understand French, this would be a completely different trip. We would probably still be at the police station trying to give those two officers descriptions of the taxi driver."

Amy smiled. "I was thinking this morning that we should take them some cookies."

"Cookies?"

"Sure. Cookies or maybe chocolate. They were nice young men. They helped us out and gave us glasses of water, remember?"

"One also offered to give you a ride on his scooter. Is that your hidden motivation, Amelie Jeanette?" The tease in my voice was evident. "Are you hoping to take him up on his offer?"

"No! You said it the other night. I'm old enough to be his mother. I just wanted to be polite and offer a motherly gesture of appreciation. That's why I came up with the idea of cookies."

Amy's reasoning made sense. She always had been the picture of graciousness.

"You tell me what you want to do," I said. "I'll follow your lead."

"Let me think about it for a little while. Let's see if we can find some more shops. I have souvenir money that's burning a hole in my pocket."

Crossing the boulevard, we headed down the opposite side of the Champs-Elysées and both shivered a little. The wind had changed. Standing on the corner talking for as long as we had chilled us. I watched the clouds barreling in from the east. Ducking into the first clothing shop we came to, Amy and I greeted the staff, and as soon as Amy asked a question in French about the sweater set in the window, the clerk turned into a helpful assistant.

Amy bought the cashmere cardigan with matching shell and pranced out of the store delighted. I was thrilled that she had found such great quality clothes and that the set fit her well. Two stores later Amy stopped to look in the window at a pink top with black trim, complete with a little black bow at the neck.

"That's you," she said.

"Me? I've never worn anything like that."

"I know. But you should. Now is the time. Come on. At least try it on."

I was sure I wouldn't like the cutesy top, but I tried it on to appease Amy. Before she had a chance to say, "Ooh la la!" I already was smiling at my reflection. I liked it. The price was twice what I would pay for a shirt at home, but with Amy's coaxing, there was no way I was going to leave the store without that Parisian top. It was evidence, like Amy's cashmere sweater set, that the two of us had fully arrived. We were buying clothes displayed in the windows on the Champs-Elysées.

I felt transformed and told Amy so. She smiled. "Voilá! We are suddenly *très chic*."

With our spirits splendidly elevated, Amy and I ventured into three more stores. None of them had anything we considered a "find," so we window-shopped the rest of the boulevard. By the time we had scoped out the last shop, Amy was looking at her watch.

"We can still make it to Napoleon's tomb."

I thought she was kidding and said, "Oh, goodie! I was hoping we would have time for that today."

Her expression let me know that unless I wanted to be left to find my way back to the hotel on foot or at the mercy of the next Parisian taxi driver who came along, I better stow my sarcasm and stick with her. I decided it was a French thing to want to visit Napoleon's tomb and looked at the map with her. The most direct route to the Invalides was via the underground Metro.

Our feet led us to down under the city at the first Metro station we came to. I had forgotten how impressive this elaborate transportation system was and how strange it felt to be walking through long well-lit tunnels underground.

Amy's French proved useful once again, as we figured out how to buy tickets and board the right train. We had no problem slipping through the sliding doors as they opened and joining the startlingly wide variety of people sitting and standing in the modern train.

"Look around," Amy whispered to me as we stood near each other, our shoulder bags in protective mode. I had fixed my gaze out the window and was watching the walls flash past as we sped to the next stop.

"Look at all the faces," Amy whispered.

I looked at the faces around us. Within our train car we had a mix of skin color, hair color, and apparel that made our group look as if we were headed to a photo shoot for an ad about honoring diversity.

When we slipped out of the train at Invalides, Amy smiled widely. "It was like heaven in there."

"Heaven?"

"Yes. All those different people. So much variety. I loved it!"

Then, as if to back up her impression of the heavenlies, music suddenly filled the hollowed-out underground tunnels. A musician stood in the center of the main connecting tunnel playing a pan flute. A woman sat beside him, a blanket wrapped around her legs and holding a small wooden bowl in her outstretched hand, soliciting donations for the free concert.

Amy stepped to the side and closed her eyes to listen. The haunting melody echoed off the tiled chamber and came back to face us. Like a lonely hitchhiker, the song was looking for a free ride out of the underground chambers. We had stopped long enough for the tune to hop in.

That's all it took for the graceful notes to settle inside our heads and catch a free ride as far as we were willing to take it. Amy placed a large bill in the wooden bowl of the music-givers and walked away humming.

We came up topside to the other world where car horns and screeching brakes created the melodies that echoed off the tall, plastered walls of the weary buildings. A fine rain fell on our faces at an angle and continued to mist us all the way to the golden dome of the Invalides museum. We toured the war museum and marched with a host of interested viewers past the tomb of Napoleon I.

I don't know if it was a memorable experience for Amy or not. We were both so weary by the time we found a nearby bistro that our dinner conversation consisted of comments on the excellent French onion soup and amazement at how much rain was now pelting the streets outside.

We were soaked by the time we hurried from the bistro to the curb, where we hailed a taxi and made sure we didn't put our shopping bags in the trunk.

The rain still was coming down in earnest when we reached our hotel and paid the taxi driver nine euros.

That's when Amy realized how much the unscrupulous driver had overcharged us for the ride from the airport.

"I'm not going to let it get to me." She turned to me in the compact elevator. "It's not worth being mad about. Thanks for not making a big deal about it, Lisa. You could have scolded me royally that first night when I overpaid him, but you didn't."

I didn't tell Amy that I'd thought about it. Wasn't that the same as actually saying something?

"Grace upon grace," Amy said as she slipped the key into our hotel room door. "That's what you have always given me."

"Actually, I would say that's what you've given me, Amy."

"You give me more."

"No, Amy, you give me more."

She laughed. "I'm not going to fight with you over which one of us is better at heaping grace upon grace. Let's just say that God is the One who pours the grace on us every day, and every now and then you and I have so much left over that we manage to share some of it with each other."

"Okay. I'll agree to that."

Upon entering our room, we found a sealed envelope that apparently had been slipped under our door while we were away. Inside was a handwritten note from the inspector who had dashed out of the hotel in pursuit of the taxi driver. As best as Amy could decipher, the inspector was asking her to call him when we returned.

"I think we better wait till morning to call," Amy said. "It's so late."

"I wonder if he wants more details." I slipped into the bathroom. "Because I don't think there's much else we could tell him. Hey, I'm going to take a shower to warm up, unless you want to take one first."

"No, I'm too tired."

By the time I emerged ready for bed, Amy already was asleep. She had the television news on low. I watched CNN for a while in the dim light, curious to see what was happening at home and in the rest of the world. It struck me that with only one station available, it could influence a viewer's opinion of world events without the person even realizing it. At home we had several news channels to choose from, so we heard various angles on the same story. I felt far from home for the first time on our trip.

I didn't miss home very much. I missed Joel but not too much. Mostly I felt privileged to be in Paris with Amy and even more privileged to experience this adventure with her in such comfort.

Wrapping the extra blanket from the closet around my shoulders, I pulled the corner chair up to the window. A wonder-world of glimmering lights filled my view. For a long time I hid behind the fold of the open drapes and watched Paris sleep.

In the solitude I thought about Gerard. I thought about my childhood. I thought about all the expectations placed on me in my early years and how diligently I had tried to follow the rules and stay off the punishment radar screen at my house. I thought about how old I was and how Amy seemed so much younger than me. She retained some sort of lovely strain of lightheartedness from our childhood while I...well, I mostly hid. Hiding felt familiar. It seemed the only way to keep from feeling overwhelmed.

Padding over to my bed, I burrowed under the covers and recalled the hitchhiking flute notes from the Metro. They played an evening serenade for me. Sleep came with a snuffer and put out all my flickering thoughts.

I woke to the sound of Amy dialing the phone.

"What time is it?" I mumbled.

"Eight o'clock, sleepyhead."

"I hope you're calling room service for a pot of coffee, Little Miss Merry Sunshine."

"No, I'm calling the inspector."

I rolled over in bed and tried to snatch another few moments of precious sleep while Amy engaged in a lengthy phone conversation accompanied by a lot of note taking on a piece of hotel stationery.

"You're not going to believe this!" Amy exclaimed after she hung up.

"Are you going to call for coffee now?" I muttered.

"Lisa, forget the coffee. You and I are heroes!"

"Good." I still hadn't opened my eyes. "When the people of Paris decide to construct a statue to commemorate our ability to be duped by a local con artist, may I pretty please pose with a cup of coffee in my hand?"

"You didn't even hear why we're heroes!" Amy came over and bounced on the end of my bed. "Wake up! Look at me. They got the guy. The inspector caught the taxi driver. He said it was because of us!"

I forced myself up on my elbows and squinted at the beaming Amy Morning Glory. "Really?"

"Yes! How's that for making our mark on this fine city?"

"We don't have to identify the guy in a lineup or anything, do we?"

"No. The inspector was calling to say that as his way of personally thanking us, he would like to treat us to dinner tomorrow night at his brother's restaurant."

I looked at Amy skeptically. "Is that normal?"

"It's a very French thing to do. I have the directions. Our reservations are for eight o'clock. So, let's get going and see what we can see between now and eight o'clock tomorrow night."

I flopped back in bed. "You call for the coffee, and I'll lie here and decide what to wear to our award ceremony."

"Come on." Amy tugged at my blankets and shone her bright mood all over me. "The day awaits us! Let's get out in it and find some breakfast. It will be something new, instead of the same old croissants and coffee."

I failed to see how scrumptious flaky croissants and splendid French roast coffee with real cream had turned into "the same old" after only two mornings. But I knew better than to argue, so I tumbled out of bed in an effort to keep up with Amy-girl. She seemed determined to kick our sightseeing up a notch and demonstrate to me how to "shake what my mama gave me." Shirleene would have been proud of her.

I, on the other hand, wanted to slip her a sleeping pill.

Twelve

I can describe our day of sightseeing with one word. Exasperating.

We ate a leisurely breakfast at a café three doors down from our hotel. The rain from the night before continued to keep the streets slick, and as a result, we witnessed a fender bender out the window. It seemed like a good day for the Louvre. And a good day for umbrellas, which we purchased from a sidewalk vendor for five euros each. Mine broke within two blocks on our way to the Louvre when a sharp wind popped it inside out. As the wind rose, the April shower turned fierce.

Huddling under Amy's umbrella, we tromped through puddles and arrived at the Louvre's entrance only to find it closed. Who closes a major museum on a Tuesday?

Chilled on the outside and slightly steamed on the

inside, we slipped into a taxi and asked to go to Montmartre. The quaint restaurants and sidewalk artists painting portraits sounded so appealing when Jill had told us about this district outside the city.

Again, we weren't thinking. Or reading our travel guides. As the driver took us through the mangle of traffic, we only managed to inch our way through the main intersections. We should have taken the Metro.

"This is ridiculous." I watched the meter click as we sat still. "Amy, would you mind trying this another day? It's cold, and we're not going to want to linger at the outdoor artists' stands. They might not even be painting today because of the weather."

"You're right." She asked the driver to turn around the first chance he got and take us to Hotel Isabella.

That minor accomplishment took forty-five minutes. I don't want to talk about how much the cab cost us.

It was almost two in the afternoon when we unlocked the door to our room. We both immediately noted that our room hadn't yet received maid service.

"I can't believe this day!" Amy dropped her wet umbrella in the corner and marched over to the phone to request the room be cleaned.

All I wanted to do was soak in a hot bath to remove the chill. Instead, I changed into my warmest sweater and a dry pair of pants. Amy changed as well and told me we needed to leave when the maid came in to clean up.

"The room isn't that bad," I said. "We can tidy it up. Just ask for some dry towels, and we'll be fine."

Amy shook her head. "I made too much of a fuss when I called down to the desk. Come on, I'll treat you to a chocolate drink at Angelina's."

I would have argued, but my defenses were down. Angelina's was close. The walkway was covered. There didn't seem much to complain about.

We sat at a small table for two next to the wall and tried to medicate our tourist ills with all the goodies that had charmed us the sunny afternoon we had spent there with Jill. Today, nothing cheered us up.

"Have you noticed how crazy everything has been on this trip?" Amy asked.

Feeling sassy I said, "Well, yeah. I've been here, too, you know."

"Drink some more chocolate," Amy said. "You're not sweetened up enough yet. All I was trying to say was that everything we've experienced is either over-the-moon spectacular or jump-off-a-cliff horrible."

"I know." I used my two thin straws to stir what remained of the chocolate. "That's Paris for you. I tried to warn you."

Amy scowled at me. "It'll get better."

We sloshed our way back to our room and spent the remainder of the stormy afternoon taking turns soaking in the bathtub. A tiny corner of my psyche said this was my fault. I knew it was ridiculous to blame myself, but that's what I did whenever frustration set in. After all, I was the one who had wanted to give Amy a sleeping pill to slow her down. I had made that silent wish, and this is what happened.

Amy turned on the television and watched *Back to the Future* in French. I slept through most of it and was thankful for a day to let my wits catch up with my body.

"Feeling better?" Amy asked, when I woke up after dark. She was curled up on the chair by the window with the tour book in her lap.

"Much better." I stretched and said nodding at the book, "I wondered why none of the tour books suggests planning a day in the schedule to adjust."

"Do you mean going 'back to the future' and adjusting the flux capacitor in one's time-space continuum?"

"What are you talking about?"

Amy laughed. "Too much TV. Hey, what do you think of taking a bus tour?"

"Tomorrow?"

"No, now. A company down the road from here offers night tours on a double-decker bus. What do you think?"

"Is it still raining?"

"Nope. Skies are clear. Stars are coming out."

"Well, in that case, we better go join them." As a night person, I was ready to get up and go. Amy-girl hadn't napped. She wouldn't know what hit her.

I bundled up, expecting to be chilled again, but the night was calm and mild. The vicious rain clouds had drifted off to pester some other city. As we left the room, Amy stuffed a box of unopened chocolate into her shoulder bag. It was our only purchase of the day from a candy store next to Angelina's.

"Expecting to do a little snacking on the tour?" I asked.

"No, these are for the boys."

I didn't know why she would take the candy she had purchased for her husband and son. "For Mark and Davy?"

"No, the boys at the police station. I wanted to give them a thank-you gift."

I sent her a motherly look over the top of my glasses. "Are you still looking for a ride on the back of a Vespa?"

"No," Amy said coyly. "Of course not. I'm being polite. I am French, you know. This is what we do."

I nodded and took note of an important fact: Amy was wearing her skinny jeans.

"Why don't we go to the police station first?" I suggested, guessing that Amy wasn't as interested in a bus tour as she had pretended to be.

"Okay."

We retraced our steps from our first night in Paris and found the enchanting tucked-away square as inviting as it had been on our first view of it. In unison we said, "We should go to that café."

Laughing at our spontaneous harmony of thought, we

linked arms, and Amy said, "After the police station."

I added, "Instead of the bus tour.'"

"Thanks for not pointing out the obvious," Amy said.

"Obvious what?"

"The obvious fact that in forty-five years my priorities haven't changed much. Boys and food always seem to make their way to the top of the list."

I laughed some more and couldn't stop smiling when we entered the police station. As soon as the young officers on night duty saw Amy and me, they snapped to attention and began talking to Amy with more animation than we had seen on our previous visit. Obviously the news of Amy's and my elevation to French heroine status had spread to the station.

She presented them with the box of chocolates, and they expressed their unworthiness with a charm that even I, the skeptic, found irresistible. Coming around to our side of the counter, the boys thanked us both with airy kisses on each cheekbone. The slender one smelled like cigarettes.

"Old enough to be their mother," I muttered to Amy with my teeth fixed in a smile.

She ignored me and gave the boys a gracious dip of her chin. With what I assumed to be words of farewell, Amy waved, and we turned to go.

The taller one stopped us. He made an appeal to Amy, looking at her with puppy dog eyes. She gleamed. I scowled. Then I pulled out my camera. I knew what was coming.

Two minutes later, I stood on the curb outside the police station, watching Amy ride off on the back of the officer's Vespa.

Her exuberant "Wheeee!" echoed down the narrow street, and I grinned at my lighthearted friend.

As they bumped over the cobblestones on their way to the café, I murmured, "Oh, Amy-girl, you are definitely shakin' what yo' mama gave you!"

I caught it all, up close, in the viewfinder of my camera. Even the fluttering scarf around her neck looked like it was having a grand time. But because I'm her best friend, I didn't press the button that would freeze-frame the view of her jolly backside for all posterity.

I wanted Amy to remember this moment the way she saw herself and not from a truth-telling photo that would shatter her fairy tale. Putting down the camera, I turned and smiled at the other officer, who was watching from the doorway with a bonbon plumping out the side of his amused cheek.

The sputtering Vespa returned sans Amelie Jeanette, and I was invited to hop on for my free ride to dinner. I put my feet on the side pegs and rested my hands on the driver's shoulders. He spoke to me, and I said, "Oui," even though I had no idea what he said. I presumed he was asking if I was ready.

With a lurch, we took off, bumping over the cobble-stones. I clenched my teeth so I wouldn't bite my tongue. He turned the corner onto a paved road and picked up speed. I realized this wasn't the way we had walked to the station.

Tapping him on the shoulder, I said, "Café, s'il vous plaît. It's the other way, isn't it?"

"Oui," he shouted back at me as he took another corner with what felt like a daring dip.

I laughed nervously. That seemed to signal to the dare-devil that I was enjoying the detour. "I wasn't trying to get you to go faster," I said. "You can take me back to the café now. Or even to the police station. I know how to get to the café from the station. The prefect? Is that what Amy called it? Hello? Are you catching any of this?"

He was grinning now. I could see the side of his smile. With another accelerated dip, he passed two cars and swerved to avoid a puddle. My heart pounded in my throat and my fingers dug into his shoulders. Just as I was summoning my most authoritative voice to command this officer to stop and let me off, we tipped around another corner and bumped onto cobblestone.

The café, lit with twinkling lights, was straight ahead. We spun as we came to a stop in front of the café entrance. There stood Amy, laughing merrily and making good use of her camera. I hoped she was capturing the I'm-going-to-get-you-for-this expression on my face.

"How much did you pay him?" I spouted.

"Nothing." Amy gave the officer a final wave and a series of giddy French words. "When you're partially responsible for the capture of a criminal, you're entitled to all kinds of perks."

"That was perky all right." I smoothed back my floofed-up hair.

"Wasn't it fun?" Amy showed me to my seat at our table. "A little joie de vivre goes a long way on a night like this."

The rest of our joyous night rolled out with calmness as we charted out a plan for the rest of our days in Paris. Amy decided she was ready to find the linen shop on Rue Cler in the morning.

"So you're not nervous about going anymore?"

"Not as nervous as I was, but I still doubt they'll be able to understand me."

"I'm telling you, Amy, you're doing great. Everyone understands you."

"We should take a gift."

"Chocolates?" I suggested.

"Maybe. I wish I'd brought something special from home. That would have been smart."

The next morning Amy was still contemplating what sort of gift to take to Madame du Bois as we got ready for our visit to Rue Cler.

"What about flowers?"

Amy nodded, letting the idea sink in. "Yes, flowers. Perfect. Why didn't we think of that earlier?"

We left the hotel after studying the map and discovering that Rue Cler was close to the Eiffel Tower. That made it easy to get there by Metro. No taxis for us today, not in the sunshine.

Walking a few short blocks to the Metro station, we noticed a difference in how the city felt now that the rain had passed and the calm night had smoothed over what the blustery wind had done the day before. Or more accurately, the difference was in how the city smelled. It was a strange combination of wet car oil evaporating on the asphalt and overzealous trees determined to sprout one new green leaf or one new pink blossom for every drop of rain received in the storm.

Leaving the busy trees to their task, Amy and I disappeared underground and surfaced again three blocks from our destination.

Finding flowers was no problem because Rue Cler turned out to be a charming street lined with specialty shops. The busy stretch was closed to motorized traffic and reflected an old world charm. It would be easy to find the linen shop on this street. The only difficult task was deciding what flowers to buy at the stand.

Amy finally selected calla lilies and purple-bearded iris with a few pink rosebuds tucked in. The merchant wrapped the generous bouquet in green paper and tied it with a ribbon. Amy thanked him twice and walked away looking like a beauty queen minus her tiara.

I pulled out my camera and called out, "Amelie!" She didn't hear me. "Amelie Jeanette!" She turned, and I snapped a great shot of her looking like the Parisian princess I always knew she was.

Several shops we passed on the Rue Cler made use of the open space in front to set up tables outside to sell their goods. One shop sold only olive oil. We dipped inside for a look and were amazed. The entire shop was a beautiful world unto itself, boasting every sort of specialty olive oil one might conjure up. We were invited to taste several of the oils by dipping a square of pita bread into the various small ceramic dishes.

"It's okay," Amy said, giving me a fun wink. "You can take a sample off these plates. These really are samples and not leftovers from previous customers."

Ignoring her teasing, I sampled each and every oil as if I were a connoisseur. The truffle oil was the most memorable. Amy translated for the shopkeeper as he explained how the truffles used in the olive oil came from the French countryside. These rare fungi were scouted out by specially trained pigs that rooted their snouts around in the earth to find the truffles.

The shopkeeper was demonstrating as he described the process to Amy. She, in turn, joined the antics as she translated the process for me. I tried hard not to laugh aloud at two adults snorting and flaring their nostrils while trying to help me appreciate the beauty of the product contained in the small bottle.

Of course I had to buy a bottle of the expensive oil after that. I thought Joel might like it, since he had asked me to bring home some interesting food items. Then I realized it was Joel's sister, Claire, who would really appreciate the gourmet truffle oil. She had a flare for the finer things in life. I bought two bottles and decided I'd give the second one to my sister-in-law with a note saying, "A gift for Claire from Rue Cler."

Amy bought four bottles of various olive oils. Each of our purchases was wrapped individually and tied with simple twine sealed with a gold label from the shop.

As we were politely saying "au revoir," Amy paused and asked about the location of the linen shop.

"He said it's near the end of the street on the right side," she translated for me as we walked to the next store. "Ooh, *miel!*" Amy looked in the window at the tiny shop that sold only honey and honey-based products. We entered and were amazed all over again at the care and craftsmanship displayed with something as simple as honey items. I bought a bar of honey soap, and Amy bought honeycomb candles and a jar of spun honey with raspberries for toast.

"I really am planning to go to the linen shop," Amy said, as we paused in front of the next store. "It's just that each shop seems to call me to step inside."

"I know. I love this one." I gazed at three crisp white blouses displayed in the window as if they were flags on a sailboat. "Look at the one in the middle. Isn't that gorgeous?"

"Let's go in for a closer look," Amy suggested.

The store sold white blouses. Only white blouses. I never thought of how many variations a simple white blouse could have. I wanted one of each. There was something honest about these white blouses. I loved blouses tucked in and blouses with the tails out. I just didn't like ironing blouses. This store presented its unique and expensive blouses so beautifully, I could almost believe they ironed themselves each morning and crawled back on their hangers.

As we had done in each store so far, Amy and I entered, made eye contact with the proprietor, said "bon jour," and Amy answered politely if the storekeeper asked if he or she could help us. We had noticed in restaurants, shops, and museums that we were treated differently from other English-speaking tourists when we tried to fit in with Parisian ways.

I asked if I might try on one of the blouses. The shopkeeper helped me by coming into the large dressing room with me. Amy sat on a padded chair in the corner, cradling her large bouquet and adding occasional comments, always in French and in English for my benefit. The blouse fit beautifully. The price tag was pinned discreetly on the inside of the cuff. It cost more than the fun pink top and much more than any blouse I'd ever bought.

"Merci," I said, slipping off the blouse and handing it to the proprietor. I loved it. Absolutely loved everything about it. But I couldn't spend that much for a blouse. It was too luxurious. Yet the sensation of the soft airy cotton lingered on my skin.

Thirteen

Amy and I paused again at the front window of the shop next door. "Have you ever seen such beautiful chocolate in all your life?" Amy exclaimed.

"No, never." And I meant it. The window display hosted various levels of golden serving dishes lined with doilies. On each doily was arranged a pageant of chocolate delicacies, and each hand-dipped bonbon was embellished with a different twist or twirl on top. The milk chocolate candies all came with a yellow line across the side. The dark chocolate treats bore a white polka dot on top. To the side was a separate display of marzipan, toffees, and caramels.

Opening the door, we breathed in the fragrance of melting chocolate that floated from the back room. A blue velvet curtain separated us from the kitchen where the delicacies were being created.

At the sound of our arrival, the blue curtain opened, and a young woman stepped out to greet us. She left the curtain open, allowing us to see the candy chef at work. He stood in front of a marble-top table that occupied the center of the small kitchen. His right hand was covered with chocolate. I watched as he dipped another nugget of candy into a copper pan filled with melted chocolate and placed it on the marble. With a steady hand he fashioned a dainty curlycue on top of the bonbon.

"Do you see that sign on the wall?" Amy asked. "It says this shop was established in 1893. I wonder if Grandmere ever came here."

"She probably did," I said, sharing in the wonder of the possibility.

"Her favorite candies were dark chocolate wafers with bits of orange inside." Switching to French, Amy asked the young woman a question.

She answered, "oui," and went to the end of the display case.

"She said dark chocolate with orange is one of the shop's specialties." Amy had tears in her eyes. "I don't know why I'm crying, except that I can't believe I'm in Paris, buying my grandmere's favorite chocolate at a shop she probably came to."

Returning with two flat wafers of dark chocolate arranged artfully on a glass dish, the woman smiled and spoke to us.

"She says the chocolates are complimentary. In honor of Grandmere."

I said, "Merci."

Amy and I went all out, selecting chocolates for our families, some friends, and us. I made special selections for Joel, knowing how much he would appreciate handmade chocolates. Our generous purchases were treated regally, with the chocolates carefully nestled in small boxes, which were sealed with gold stickers and each wrapped with a dainty satin ribbon tied in a perfectly balanced bow.

Exiting with our revered chocolates carefully sequestered in handled shopping bags, Amy said softly, "Don't you feel as if we need to whisper so we don't wake up our sleeping candies?"

I laughed. "What would Grandmere think of us now?"

"She would be smiling."

I nodded. "Yes, she would. I loved your grandmere, Amy. Have I ever told you that?"

"I'm sure you have. I loved her, too."

"The way she looked at me…" I tried to find the words to express how I felt. "Well, she captured my heart. I always felt as if I were a dandelion child, and she was just dying to take a deep breath and send all the airy strands of my blond flyaway hair off to the four corners of the earth. She made me feel like I was her wish."

"Ooh, Lisa, that is the sweetest thing anyone has ever said about Grandmere!"

I teared up. "I guess in a small way, her wish for me is coming true. I've been blown to one of the four corners of the earth, and here she is, with us in a gentle memory."

"Okay." Amy wiped a tear. "Not fair. You got me crying. Right when I was about to go into the next shop."

I looked up and saw the sign for the next store. The Linen Shoppe. We both composed ourselves and drew in a deep breath of sunshine kissed with fresh air.

"This is it, Amelie."

"I know. Stay beside me."

"Don't worry. I will. I'm with you all the way."

A small bell sounded our arrival as I closed the heavy door behind us.

"Bon jour," Amy said to an older woman who was folding linen dish towels behind a mahogany counter.

"Bon jour," I repeated.

The woman asked Amy the usual question in French that I was beginning to recognize. Were we looking for anything in particular?

Still carrying the large bouquet in her arms, Amy walked over to the woman. Pulling out Grandmere's letter from her shoulder bag, Amy handed the missive to the woman, who reached for a pair of half-glasses on the counter. She read without moving her lips. Amy and I watched her eyebrows slowly rise. Her mouth formed a small "o" and out came a tender "ooh."

Amy grinned shyly.

The woman's words came rushing over us. She introduced herself as Norene and indicated we were to wait while she went upstairs. A few moments later she returned, cheeks rosy, and invited us to follow her up the stairs. We entered a spacious, second-floor apartment where Oriental rugs covered the wood floor. An elegant light fixture hung from the center of the ceiling.

Sitting on straight back chairs with tufted seats and polished wooden legs, Amy and I waited in the grand parlor. I felt as if we had stepped back in time. If this was the home where Grandmere had first picked up a needle and thread, as her letter had said, then I found it easy to believe this could have been the chair she sat in to begin her sewing lessons.

Norene said something to Amy and then stepped into an adjoining room.

"She says her mother is eager to meet me," Amy translated. "She's getting some pictures to show us."

"Amy," I said in a low voice, "please don't feel as if you have to translate everything for me. This is your moment. I'm thrilled to be here, but I want you to enter in without having to flip back and forth to keep me in the loop."

Amy looked relieved. "Are you sure you're okay with that?"

I nodded, content to be the wallflower.

Amy mouthed the words, "Thank you, Lisa," as Norene returned with an ornate tray holding a crystal carafe and four beautiful cut crystal glasses. She continued speaking to Amy, occasionally turning to nod in a polite effort to include me in the conversation. I nodded back as Norene poured the special offering into the crystal glasses, which signified a moment of celebration, I was sure.

We heard heavy steps approaching. Amy rose from her seat as a thick-ankled woman with fabulous white hair entered the room like a Grand Sovereign. I stood as well.

The woman wore an embroidered shawl around her shoulders. The rich shade of blues and golds in the handiwork blended in with the furniture. Coming to us with open arms, she kissed us both, starting with the right cheek and then the left. Her fragrance was extraordinary. I felt as if we had stepped into a scene from one of the works of art that we had seen at the Musée d'Orsay. Any moment a ballerina could enter this room. Nothing would surprise me.

Amy offered the bouquet of flowers to Madame du Bois. She appeared honored. At first Amy seemed to be trying very hard to remember her manners and her French words as Norene pointed to the letter, and Madame du Bois nodded her understanding. Then we sat down, and I watched Amy fall into a more relaxed communication rhythm. Soon the three women were exchanging long strings of French words with as much delight and reverence as if they were exchanging strings of pearls and then admiring them around the other's neck.

Madame du Bois handed Amy a small framed picture

of seven young girls, all wearing 1920s-style straight dresses with dropped waists and wide sashes around the area that separated the elongated bodice from the pleated skirt. Several of the girls wore big bows in their hair. Other girls wore stylish hats or had bobbed hair with curls at their jawlines.

They were a fashionable bunch. No doubt Grandmere was among them. Although when Amy handed the picture to me, I couldn't guess which one she was.

"This was a group of girls who were in a sewing class led by Madame du Bois's mother," Amy told me. "The class was held here, in this house. Can you believe that? The picture was taken in front of the linen shop." Amy drew in to take a closer look and pointed to the girl with the straight posture right in the middle.

"That's Grandmere," she said confidently. "I've seen two other pictures of her at this age, and that's definitely Grandmere."

Norene rose and carried the tray of refreshments to us, offering it to Amy first and then to me. I said, "Merci," and received the beverage. The cut crystal felt weighty in my hand. It was old. Opulent. I wondered how many births, engagements, and anniversaries had seen the filling and clinking of these beautiful glasses.

Madame du Bois offered the toast, the joyous French words rolling off her thick tongue. I was sure she was saying something substantial and nurturing. I didn't think about how I was breaking my forty-five-year moratorium on all things alcoholic. Rather, I took the smallest of sips and let the deep-textured, amaretto-laced beverage spread over my tongue like a fine linen tablecloth, setting the palate for a banquet.

I thought of Amy's mom. She should have been here; this was the sort of moment she esteemed. This was the sort of joie de vie she had demonstrated to me as a child when she had served me pink Hostess Sno Balls on a hand-painted plate. I was surreptitiously taking her place with Amy today and felt determined to make Grandmere proud.

I sat up straighter and pulled back my shoulders. Today, more than any day in my life, I wanted to be an honorary DuPree woman.

Norene slipped in and out of the room several times. Each time she returned with a plate of simple but beautifully presented food. First came a bowl of freshly washed strawberries and a small ramekin of sugar for dipping the strawberries. Next she brought a round of goat cheese. Then the last plate included a decorative knife, a fan of crackers, and a dark spread.

"Pâté." Amy raised her eyebrows appreciatively.

Knowing full well that I was being offered goose liver, I spread a modest amount of the pâté on a cracker and took a bite. The flavor made my taste buds stand up and do a little cancan dance on my tongue.

Amy asked how I liked it. The du Bois women waited for my response. I said the first appropriate thing I could think. "Ooh la la!"

The women smiled and offered me more goat cheese. I silently congratulated myself for passing International French Diplomacy 101 with such an easy final exam. I felt honored to be a guest in the fabulous room with such charming women. I knew Amy couldn't possibly be more pleased with what she was experiencing.

Our visit lasted a little more than two hours. As the conversation wound down, Madame du Bois rose and offered Amy and me fragrant kisses on each cheek. We returned the gesture and followed Norene downstairs. I noticed that Norene had put up the closed sign on her shop door while we had been upstairs celebrating.

Before she opened her doors again to the public, Norene turned to us. "My mother and I would like you to select anything from our store as a memory to take with you."

I shouldn't have been stunned that she spoke perfect English, but I was. I realized that probably Madame du Bois spoke English as well. But this was their home. Amy had honored them by speaking their language, and no doubt she had endeared herself to them as a result. She had done what Grandmere had asked. She had blessed the du Bois family that afternoon.

"Thank you," I said to Norene. "Merci. You have been very kind and generous to us."

"You brought joy to my mother. I am the one who offers a thank-you."

Amy and I took our time, viewing the amazing assortment of fine French linens. We had observed in the other shops that the French considered it impolite to finger everything while looking, so we put our hands to our sides and used our eyes to evaluate the rows of bedsheets and stacks of tea towels.

I selected a striped tea towel for my kitchen. Norene insisted I take two. I tried to decline, but Amy gave me a firm look from across the room, and I relented. As Norene expertly wrapped the matching tea towels in tissue paper and tied the flat bundle with a raffia ribbon, I told her that every time I used the towels I would think of her, her mother, and their beautiful shop and home.

She looked pleased.

However, she was much more pleased when Amy took a bold step, went all out, and decided to take home a complete set of sheets. I was stunned. I didn't think selecting something so expensive would be polite. Norene, however, looked as if Amy was paying her a compliment by wanting the nicest quality linen in the store.

It was all so fitting. Amy went after life wholeheartedly. She always had.

In a further gesture of generosity, Norene insisted on shipping the gift home for Amy so she wouldn't have to pack the thick set in her suitcase.

With addresses exchanged, more airy kisses on the cheeks, and a potpourri of French and English farewells, Amy and I stepped out the door into the *plein air*.

"Well?" I grinned at my radiant friend. "That was wonderful."

"Yes, wonderful." Amy murmured. "So wonderful."

"Would you mind if we did a little backtracking?" I asked.

"Sure. Where do you want to go?"

"Back to the blouse shop."

Amy looked surprised. "Change your mind?"

I nodded. "Every now and then it's good to be a little extravagant and celebrate life, don't you think?"

"Absolutely. Especially when the last time I remember your being extravagant was seventeen years ago."

I tried to remember what I'd bought seventeen years ago and couldn't recall the memory that Amy seemed to have at her fingertips.

"For Jeanette. At the hotel room. Don't you remember the huge basket with all the gifts? That was immensely generous of you."

I remembered how much I'd hesitated and second-guessed myself that day. "It's not easy to break through the money barrier after growing up celebrating frugality."

"True," Amy agreed. "And it's not easy breaking through the discipline barrier when sugar is practically a daily food group. But you know what? We're getting better, you and me. We're finding a little balance in life."

I wasn't quite ready to pat myself on the back. I hadn't bought the blouse yet.

Fourteen

The shopkeeper at the blouse store recognized Amy and me and seemed surprised to see us when we entered. She switched to English when I said I had returned to buy the blouse I had tried on. She asked if we had gone far before returning to her shop.

"No," Amy said. "We've been at the linen shop. Madame du Bois's mother taught my grandmere to sew."

The shopkeeper's face burst into a smile followed by many friendly words in French. We left her shop twenty minutes later with my new blouse wrapped in tissue and cradled in a silver box with a white ribbon around it.

"She really didn't have to give me that discount," I told Amy. "I was prepared to pay the full price."

"I know. I think she wanted to do something nice since we were friends with the du Boises. It wasn't a very big discount. You probably saved a total of ten dollars. Maybe fifteen."

"Still, it was kind of her."

"Then just receive it and be blessed," Amy said.

We walked with our shopping bags tapping against our legs. Part of me struggled with feeling as if the expensive blouse, discount and all, was something I shouldn't have splurged on. This whole trip was such an extravagant gift. The rich experiences were enough in and of themselves.

It was the first time I remembered admitting to myself that I had a hard time receiving gifts. I was fine with giving and doing for everyone else, usually in moderation, but nevertheless with a willingness to help out. Receiving was a different story. Something deep inside whispered that I didn't deserve anything extra.

"Where are we going?" Amy suddenly asked.

I shook off my inner contemplations and looked around. We were heading toward the Eiffel Tower, as if a magnetic force were pulling us closer. "I wasn't paying attention. I just started walking. But since we're so close to the Eiffel Tower, let's take a few pictures."

Amy agreed, and we kept walking. And walking. The crazy part about the Eiffel Tower is that it's so huge it looks as if you could reach it in no time. But our little trek took half an hour.

We snapped each other's pictures during our approach,

upon our arrival, and again from the center looking straight up. The structure looked different in the afternoon light. Amy said it seemed rickety and not romantic, like it had at night. I thought it looked sincere. And aging.

"We have plenty of time before our eight o'clock dinner." I nodded toward the line at the ticket booth. "Are you ready to go up?"

Amy laughed. "I'm not going up there."

"Yes you are."

"No I'm not.

"Amy, it's the Eiffel Tower."

She glared at me.

"You know? Paris? Pair-ee? The Eye-full Tow-er. I really, really, really think you should go up."

"Well I really, really, really don't think I want to." Her hands were on her hips now, and she was getting her sass going. Shirleene's influence was showing up loud and clear.

With my hands on my hips, I tried to menacingly shake what my mama gave me. "Amy-girl," I raised my voice, "you are going up this thing, and you are going up it now!"

Amy stared at me. "What in the world was that?"

"Nothing." I put my hands down and silenced my rhythm-challenged hips. Switching quickly to what I hoped was psychology, I said, "You have one question to ask yourself. That question is, how can I go home from Paris and tell people I was this close but didn't go up the Eiffel Tower?"

"Easy. I just say I went *to* the Eiffel Tower. I don't have to say I went *up* the Eiffel Tower."

"You have to do this."

"No I don't."

"Amy, I understand your fear of heights, and I respect that. But this backing down thing is not like you. You are a woman who faces challenges with gusto. I saw the way you gave birth to your babies. And look at how you conquered your weight in less than a year."

"I never hit my goal. I still had six pounds to lose when we left home. So you can't say I exactly conquered my weight."

"Six pounds? Amy, we've walked off six pounds since we've been here. At least. Forget about the six pounds. What about the fifty pounds you lost before we came?"

"Forty-nine," she corrected me.

"Forty-nine! Forty-nine, Amy! That's a huge victory! You went after a gigantic goal, and you not only met it, you conquered it. That's what you do. You fight for what matters to you. You are my Joan of Arc. You can't walk away now. This is it. The Eiffel Tower. You need to go up there and make peace with your fear of heights."

Amy looked at me defiantly. "Why?"

"Otherwise you will spend the rest of your life telling yourself that you had the chance to scale the one and only Eiffel Tower and look down over all of Paris and conquer this thing. But you didn't do it. And I know you well enough to know that *that* isn't something you will want to live with."

Amy crossed her arms. "I hate that you know me so well."

"Yeah, well, I do. And sometimes I hate it that you can see right through me, too. But that's why we have each other, Amy. What did Jill say we were? Sisterchicks? Yeah, we're Sisterchicks. And I'm telling you as your Sisterchick that you need to leave this city with no regrets. Believe me, you do not want to leave here with memories that will haunt you the rest of your life."

My voice had elevated. A couple walking past looked over at us. I took it down a notch and said, "Just promise me something. I've made lots of promises to you. This is what I want you to promise me. Promise me, Amelie Jeanette DuPree Rafferty, that you will not leave Paris with regrets. No regrets. Promise me."

She paused before nodding her head slowly. "Okay. But the same goes for you, Lisa Marie Kroeker Moreland. No regrets like last time."

Her words sliced my heart with the precision of a surgeon's blade. In my typical duck-and-cover routine, I pulled out a diverting surprise. "Amy, my middle name is not Marie."

"What?"

"It's not Marie."

"Yes it is. You told me your middle name was Marie when we met in third grade."

"No. Actually, *you* told me my middle name was Marie, and I didn't correct you. I liked Marie better than my real middle name."

Amy's hands were back on her hips, and her mouth was open. "So what is your middle name?"

"Mona."

"Mona. Mona? Your middle name is Mona? That's not so bad. All these years you let me believe your middle name was Marie because you didn't want me to know your name was Mona?"

"I didn't want anyone to know. It was another one of my father's little jokes."

"And what is so all-fire funny about the name Mona?"

I gave Amy a come-on-work-with-me-here look. Apparently I had to do the math for her. "Think about it. How would you like to grow up being Lisa Mona Kroeker."

"Ooh. Lisa Mona. I get it."

"You renamed me that day on the school ground, Amy. And I let you." My voice, tone, and posture softened. "It was the first time anyone accessorized me with hope. Sorry if I wore it too long."

I didn't know if Amy was going to laugh or cry.

She did a wonderful thing. She opened her arms and wrapped me in the accessory that is even more versatile and lovely than hope—she wrapped me in acceptance. Grace upon lovely layer of grace.

"Your dad..." she muttered under her breath.

"I know." I pulled away and blinked back a rogue tear.

"You do know, don't you, that I named my daughter Jeanette Marie for the two of us?"

"What do you mean?"

"Jeannette because of my middle name and Marie for what I thought was your middle name."

I felt as if the bottom had dropped out of my stomach. "I always thought it was Jeanette for your grandmere and…I guess I never knew where you came up with the Marie. Oh, Amy, now I feel awful."

"Well, you should," Amy said with a snit in her voice, giving the end of my flyaway hair a flick of her fingers. "But I'm not going to change her name now. Not to Jeanette Mona. I would never do that to a daughter of mine. I can't believe your dad did that. Or, actually, yes I can believe it. Lisa, I'm sorry."

"Why are you sorry? I'm the one who's sorry. I should have told you years ago. It was too painful to admit in elementary school. You know how cruel kids are, making fun of other people's names. By the time you and I reconnected, it didn't seem to matter. I had no idea you named Jeanette after me."

"We're pathetic, you know that?" Amy said. "Come on. We need to go someplace else."

"Where?"

"I don't care. We just need to leave and come back here another day. I'm not ready to sort through any more of your childhood trauma or my fear of heights. The Eiffel Tower will still be here tomorrow."

Amy linked her arm through mine. "When we get home, I'm driving you to the county courthouse or wherever we need to go, and you are going to change your middle name."

"You mean legally change it to Marie?"

"You can change it to anything you want. Just make the Mona go away."

"Fine." I sounded snippy but secretly agreed with Amy and appreciated her nudge.

"You know what I think we should do now?" Amy asked.

"It's obviously not going to the top of the Eiffel Tower."

"I think we should go to the Louvre and see the real Mona."

"You are such a brat."

"No, I'm not. I'm trying to make up for lost time yesterday. The book said all the wings are open until midnight tonight."

"I suppose that's to make up for being closed on Tuesdays?"

Amy shrugged. "All I know is, we have almost five hours before we go to dinner. We can find the Louvre easily by Metro, and it's close enough to our hotel that we can change before we go to the restaurant."

"What are we waiting for?"

I asked the same question of Amy again half an hour later. We were standing in a sea of people in front of the glass pyramid dome that marked the escalator entrance to the Louvre.

"They're checking through everyone's bags before we can enter," Amy said.

I adjusted my shopping bags and watched the glass circular elevator that rose in the center interior of the glass pyramid. "I hope they don't unpack all our gifts."

"Or confiscate our chocolates," Amy added.

Once again, her familiarity with French came to our aid because she was able to explain where we had bought the items we were lugging around with us. The guards checked only our purses and waved us through into the museum. At the base of the pyramid, we stood in another line to buy entrance tickets.

Entering the Louvre was completely different from when I had been there last. Feeling as if we were lining up to enter an amusement park, I hoped the humongous museum of priceless art hadn't gone commercial.

Within the first few minutes inside the actual museum, I realized little had changed. I soon found myself lost in wonder as Amy and I strolled quietly side by side, consulting our guide book.

Standing in front of a statue from 1513 titled *Rebellious Slave*, Amy read, "'Michelangelo said his purpose was to carve away the marble in order to reveal that which God put inside. In this example of Renaissance mastery, the subject seems to be struggling to free himself of the rock he's made from.'"

She tilted her head appreciatively at the statue. "We can all relate, can't we?"

"Relate to what?" I asked, awed by the fine details in the statue.

"I relate to being a rebellious slave to my old self. Don't all of us struggle constantly to be free from the elements we're made of?"

I gave Amy a surprised look. "That was profound."

She ignored me and kept moving forward, following the signs to the Mona Lisa. I thought of the sensations I'd felt the first time we went to Angelina's. I saw myself as the rebel in an orderly universe where there are no "maverick molecules." Gravity always works.

If God was the True Artist, creating all of us and this world filled with intricate details, what was He thinking? What was He feeling? What was He trying to express? What does He carve away from us to release what He put inside?

"Amy?" I stopped in a long hallway of framed artwork. "I have a question. What do you think God was thinking when He made us?"

"Easy. He was thinking He wanted us."

That had not been my conclusion. "Why do you say that?"

"Because that's what He says over and over in the Bible. He wants us to be in a restored relationship with Him. Why are you asking?"

Amy made it sound so simple. I'd spent my life viewing God and His commands as complicated. I knew all about the struggle to break free from the rock I'd come from.

"Just thinking," I said to Amy.

We worked our way down another long corridor in this converted palace where Napoleon once ruled. Our plan was to get in line to see Mona Baby and then back-track with as much time as we had left to view other key pieces, such as the Venus de Milo.

The crowds thickened the closer we got to the small gallery where the portrait of Mona Lisa was framed by seri-ous-faced guards on either side. Amy and I shuffled single file through the roped-off section where the small, dark painting waited for us to take our thirty-second glimpse.

Mona Lisa was frozen, unmoving, with that evocative smile of hers. She hadn't moved in twenty-three years, and neither had I. We were both stuck. Something had frozen in me in this place, in Paris. Something deep inside. Mona Lisa was stuck where she was and so was Lisa Mona.

This is the part of the story I hesitate to tell. I started to cry. Not sobbing or a *whaa-whaa*-spoiled-little-girl sort of crying but a deep down weeping. Inside me a wall crumbled. When it came tumbling down, the tears rolled out steadily without a sound.

Fifteen

After we were past the mobs of Mona Lisa gawkers and in a side room, Amy noticed I was crying. *Leaking* was a more accurate description. The long-stuffed emotions forged a stream down my face.

"Lisa?"

I turned away and wiped my cheeks with the back of my hand.

"Lisa, what is it? You aren't crying about your middle name, are you? The Lisa Mona thing? Is that what got to you?"

"No." I sniffed and offered a small fake smile.

"What's going on?"

I lied to Amy. I hate that I did that. But I said, "Nothing."

Since she was so great about respecting all my stop signs, she said, "Okay." And she didn't probe further.

The crazy part was I wanted her to probe. I wanted her to burrow inside this sudden crevice in the wall around my heart. I wanted her to break through, working with her bare hands, pulling off the chipped parts to reveal what was hidden inside. I wanted all my tears and fears to be liberated. I wanted to be free. I wanted Amy to do that for me without being asked or directed.

Instead, she suggested we go through the French Revolution section of paintings. We did, but I don't remember a thing. I kept thinking about what a mess I was inside. What a hypocrite. What a big, fat liar. I was miserable.

The rest of the afternoon was a blur of colors, shapes, and textures. I floated through the Louvre, thinking the whole time. Thinking, remembering, evaluating, and sometimes crying a little more. I was stuck, and I knew it, but I didn't see how to get unstuck. I tried to stuff my pain back inside—only deeper—so it would have less of a chance to leak out.

So that's what I did. I stuffed. Healing myself, I didn't know how to do. Stuffing, I did.

By dinnertime I had pulled myself together and hoped I wouldn't ruin our experience at the fancy restaurant.

"What a quaint corner of Paris," Amy said, when our taxi let us out on the corner of Saint Michael's. "I wonder why they call it the Latin Quarter? It doesn't have a Spanish sort of feel to me."

"It's because of the university," I said. "The students

used to speak Latin. For hundreds of years students sat at the outdoor cafés in this area."

"Oh, that Latin. Have you been here before? Do you remember this section?"

"Yes."

Amy studied my response. I knew what she was looking for. Any hint of "him" on my face. All the memory starters were here. His apartment was close. The small, third-story closet that used to be his apartment. His apartment and…

Rounding a corner, my memory told my eyes to look to the left. Reluctantly, I peeked, and there it was. Just as I remembered it. The brightly lit sidewalk café where I had given away my heart. Not piece by piece like a cautious woman. No. I was twenty-two that magical summer, and I handed my heart over whole and tender and pounding.

Gerard!

Amy stopped walking. An expression borne of deep love for me and for our friendship showed on her face. She tilted her head. "Gerard?"

"Did I say that aloud?"

"Yes, you just said, 'Gerard.'"

Not once in the last two decades had I said anything about Gerard to anyone. Had my thoughts begun to leak out now in whispers?

"Is that his name?"

I slowly nodded. A fine silky rain began to mist us as

we stood in the middle of a swirl of pedestrians on the cobblestone pathway.

"Yes, his name was Gerard."

Just like that I handed over the password to my past to my best friend. And for all my efforts to remain sealed up, the truth was, I wanted her to have it. I wanted her to use it well. I trusted her.

With disarming irreverence for my sacred secret, Amy simply said, "All these years I thought his name would have been Bob."

"Bob?"

"Bob or Mike or some other clearly American name. I never guessed he was French." With that, she turned and headed for our restaurant.

Standing alone in the middle of my drama-soaked memories, I realized Amy wasn't afraid of my story the way I was. She knew there had been a "him." She knew that from the first time I told her I didn't like Paris and didn't want to return. She knew, and yet she hadn't pushed me to tell. Now that she knew, she refused to bow to the inappropriate shrine I had constructed for this man. This altar in my heart was about to be disassembled, and I would soon be set free. I just knew it.

All I had to do was give her my story.

"Amy?"

She didn't hear me. She was already half a block away. I hurried to catch up to where she stood in front of a small wooden door with the number 14 over the doorpost. If she wasn't feeling rushed to hear about Gerard right then, I could wait, too.

The window beside the door was framed with lace curtains. The inside appeared to be lit only by candlelight.

"I think this is the restaurant," she said.

"Are you sure? It looks like a home. It's so small."

"This is what he said. Number 14. Let's try the door and see if it opens."

"Amy," I cautioned. If it was someone's home, I would have thought it would be a good idea to knock first.

But Amy pushed on the latch, and the door easily opened. This was her night for trying closed doors and boldly walking right in.

A short man in a dark vest stood by one of the six candlelit tables and welcomed us with cool reserve. Amy explained who we were, and the greeting changed to match the warm glow of the room. We were shown to a table set with sparkling crystal. Only one other couple was seated in the restaurant at the opposite end.

Everything about this haven from the rain spoke of Old World elegance and charm: the intimacy of the seating plan, the dark woods, the amber candlelight, the crisp white table linen. I felt as if we had been invited to a special banquet in our honor.

When Amy extracted a few more details from our waiter, we were surprised to find he was the owner as well as the only waiter of this petite restaurant. He was the inspector's brother, and we were to order whatever we wished, as the inspector's guests. However, the inspector would not be joining us. Business detained him, but he wished for us to enjoy the dinner.

"What do you think?" I whispered. "Should we stay?"

"Of course. We were invited."

Amy took the chair offered to her. I took the one across from her, and our extravagant dining experience began. The waiter spoke to us discreetly, apparently describing our dinner options. We gazed at a printed menu, but it seemed more important to listen to his suggestions regarding the specialties of the house.

As Amy began to translate the options, I told her to go ahead and order for me. I'd be happy with whatever she chose.

"Great idea." Amy turned to the waiter. She asked him something, and he seemed to come alive. The two of them carried on a lengthy tête-à-tête.

"What did you order?"

"I have no idea." Amy grinned. "I went with your suggestion. I said something like, 'My friend and I would be honored to have whatever you recommend.' I think he said we're having seven courses. He might have said five. He has an accent."

"Oh, really?" I grinned at what I thought was Amy's attempt at a joke.

"No, I'm serious. His French pronunciation is different. It's not Parisian. He must be from another part of France. I was just starting to understand a fair amount of what the locals were saying, and now this guy has me wishing I had a dictionary with me."

"I'm sure it will be delicious whatever it is."

Amy glowed. This was the Paris she had long dreamed of; we were partaking of the finer things this city had to offer.

I told myself not to do anything to embarrass her or to ruin the ambience. This was not the time or place to tell her about Gerard. But she had the password now. She knew his name. Even that small piece lifted from my heart made me feel a little lighter.

We talked in low voices about the various small pictures in dark wooden frames on the wall. Bottles of Badoit mineral water were opened at our table and served with a flourish. Our cloth napkins were removed from the table, flapped open, and laid across our laps for us. Amy kept smiling.

After a light salad of mixed greens was served with a flavorful dressing, the next course placed before us swam in melted butter and garlic. The waiter announced the delicacy, and I looked to Amy for translation.

With a straight face, she said, "Frog legs."

Something deep in my psyche rejected anything toad- or frog-related. "Amy, please don't take this the wrong way, but I can't do this. I can't eat these. I can't even look at them. Just the word *frog* makes me smell car wash wax and see a flashing neon toad sign."

Amy laughed and suggested I look the other way while she downed the rare treat.

The third course, a simple presentation of white asparagus tips decorated with a dark yellow swirl of sauce around the rim of the plate, helped me forget all about the frog legs. I finally relaxed and settled in, realizing we had no place to go and nothing to do but spend the rest of the night dining. I'd never felt so enveloped inside a dining experience before.

When the waiter set the main course before us, I looked at the pretty picture it created for a moment before picking up my fork. White pieces of fish with a yummy-smelling sauce nestled inside a fan-shaped seashell like babies in a bassinet. Cuddled up next to the seashell on the plate was a whole, cooked onion stuffed with creamy-looking rice. Basil and a hint of sage rose on the steam from the dish.

"Ooh." Amy pointed to the fish. "Coquilles St. Jacques!"

Seeing the uncomprehending look on my face, she added, "Sea scallops, Lisa, cooked in an herbed butter sauce and topped with Swiss cheese. It's a classic French dish."

The first piece I put in my mouth made me close my

eyes and chew slowly like a connoisseur of all seafaring delicacies. The scallops almost melted in my mouth. I knew my taste buds would remember this experience forever.

Amy tried to express her tandem enjoyment, but all she could say was, "My mouth is so happy!"

We laughed, and I looked over my shoulder. The other couple in the restaurant seemed oblivious to us and our laughter. Around us floated contented sounds: forks tapping the edge of knives, sparkling clinks of crystal stemware being lifted and returned to the table, simmering sounds of delicacies being prepared in the tiny kitchen behind the cutout window, cello music rolling out the low mellow notes of a melancholy heart from the speaker behind the small lamp with a burgundy shade. We were sequestered in a pocket of time where the rest of the world faded away.

"So," Amy said, sliding into my thoughts with an equally slow-measured pace. "His name was Gerard, was it?"

I couldn't believe how calm I felt. "Yes, Gerard. That was his name."

"And?"

"And…how much do you want to hear?"

I thought she would say, "Everything." I thought that's what I wanted. What I needed. It would have been typical of Amy to say, "Tell me everything." But we weren't in a typical place. And we weren't gluttons. We were in a place where only a little was sufficiently satisfying when prepared and served with expertise.

All Amy said was, "I want to hear about what happened in your heart the last time you were in Paris."

I began my story with, "Well, I was young, he was charming, and…"

"And you were in Paris." Amy swished her hand as if that fact explained everything.

"Yes, I was in Paris, but…"

Amy looked at me with an expression of acceptance. I knew I could tell her anything. I took a courageous breath and plunged in.

"The other girls I was traveling with flew home a week before I did. Originally I was going to go back to London and stay at the same place where we stayed the first four days of our trip. But then I met Gerard. At the tour office. He sold my girlfriends and me tour tickets for a day trip to Versailles, and then he turned out to be our guide."

I told Amy how much fun we had that day. I told her how Gerard wasn't like any other man I'd ever met, so sure of himself and so quick to express what he was feeling.

"He turned down our group offer to take him out for coffee after our tour of the palace at Versailles. But he whispered to me that I was the enchanting one and kissed me on the neck."

"The enchanting one," Amy repeated. "Suave."

"He definitely was suave. The next morning my friends

and I were leaving the youth hostel, ready to go our separate ways. Across the street I saw Gerard. He came toward us with his hands behind his back and his eyes fixed on me. Then he held out a single red rose and said, 'One more day, Lisa.' I stayed one more day and that turned into two days and…"

"You fell helplessly, hopelessly in love." Amy smiled, as if I were telling her a fairy tale.

"Yes," I heard myself say. "I fell in love with him. Hopelessly, helplessly, completely."

Rolling my shoulders back and drawing in another deep breath I said, "Oh, that felt good."

Amy lowered her chin. "Did you never admit that to yourself before?"

"No. At least never aloud."

Amy reached across the table and squeezed my hand. "Then keep going. Keep telling yourself the truth, Lisa."

I leaned back in my chair, and that seemed to be the signal for our waiter to bring the next course. He smoothly presented us each with a small aperitif glass of lemon sorbet to clear our palate before the dessert.

Then he set a copper sauté pan of cherries in the center of the table and sparked the delicacy in flames. Amy and I "oohed" in unison and watched the fire quickly dissipate. The cherries jubilee was served with dark coffee in a silver pot that had a long, elegant pour spout. A plate of fine cheese was placed in front of us, but the strong smell made both of us turn away. To be polite, we tried a small taste of each piece, and then gave our waiter a slightly desperate look. He returned and removed the plate of cheese as a gracious gesture to our unappreciative taste buds.

As he poured another cup of strong coffee for both of us, he made it clear that we weren't being rushed but rather invited to linger as long as we wanted at our secluded table.

During our dessert, I had considered what to tell Amy. I knew I could spend the rest of the night giving her little details of how Gerard and I strolled for long hours along the Seine and sat at sidewalk cafés on the Champs-Elysées, sipping coffee and holding hands. None of those details seemed necessary. She got the point. I fell in love. This conversation seemed more for my benefit than hers.

I reentered my tale by telling her the first thing that came to my mind. "Gerard said I was strange."

"Strange?"

"His English was fluent, but there were a few glitches. I think he meant *different* or *unique*. At least that's what I told myself. My views of life were so different from his. The second time we went out for coffee I arm-wrestled him to see who was going to pay. He said French girls never arm-wrestled."

"Did you tell him that not many French girls grew up with brothers like yours?"

"Yes." I brushed a few crumbs off the linen tablecloth

and smiled. "I won the arm wrestling, so he had to pay. Then I told him I could take him in leg wrestling, too, but I never proved it."

"Leg wrestling, huh?" Amy's eyebrows asked all the questions that I knew were inevitable.

"We never did, just so you know."

"You never leg-wrestled? Or you never went to bed together?"

"Neither. I told Gerard that if what we were feeling for each other was real, then it would last. You know how cautious I was. I told him I was saving myself for my husband. He never had heard that before from a woman. I think my morals intrigued him at first. That was part of what made me strange."

"And also made you so attractive to him. He fell in love with you, too, didn't he?"

"I don't know. I thought so. But it couldn't have been real. It didn't last."

"Oh, it lasted, all right," Amy said. "We're talking about him now, aren't we? I'd say he's still in your life."

I wasn't prepared for her comment. Yet she was right. This man had never completely left me. I carried around his memories secretly, sacredly, in my heart. That realization made me feel sick to my stomach. I did what I always did when the shame-beast pounced on me. I defended myself.

"I honestly thought what I felt for Gerard was real. I

mean, real enough for what I understood about love and life and myself at that age."

"I'm sure it was real. There's no shame in that."

"Yes, but Amy, I look back now, and when I'm honest with myself, I see that I could have so easily given myself to him."

"You did."

"No, I just told you. We didn't go to bed together. We were more than a little familiar, if you know what I mean, but I didn't give myself to him."

Amy looked at me with a very grown-up version of the same expression she had given me the summer night under the pink canopy of her bed when she told me where babies came from. "You did give yourself to him, Lisa. You gave Gerard your heart. You fell in love with this man. Truly. Sleeping with someone doesn't somehow make your love authentic."

I had no response. All these years the only comfort in my memories of Gerard was that I'd done the right thing by staying on this side of virginity. I had left Paris with a broken heart but with my morals still intact. Yet Amy was right. I'd given Gerard the freshest, most vulnerable and eternal part of me, and he had rejected it. I'm not sure I ever gave that part of myself away entirely again. Not even to my wonderful husband.

I leaned back, stunned to realize how guarded I had been in all my relationships. I loved and gave and confided in the small circle of those closest to me. But I'd never entered in emotionally at the same level I so willingly had with Gerard.

This was staggering news. It meant that I had successfully guarded myself by taking only the smallest and most predictable steps in my relationships. The result was that I was rarely hurt. Rarely disappointed. And rarely as happy or alive as I'd been that one week with Gerard. It seemed as if I'd only half-lived.

Sixteen

"This is really hard," I told Amy, sinking into my chair at the tiny restaurant and dabbing the corners of my eyes with the cloth napkin.

"You're doing great." Amy leaned in compassionately. "Don't run from this now. I've waited years for this conversation, Lisa. Please don't shut down. Please. You're almost there. Keep telling yourself the truth."

The tears were coming in a steady stream now. "The truth really hurts," I whispered.

"I know. It also really heals." Amy sat across from me like the Rock of Gibraltar. I knew that nothing I told her would change her view of me or alter our friendship. She was the picture of grace upon grace. All I had to do was tell myself the truth. I strung the words together in my mind and let them trail out of my mouth for the first time ever.

I told Amy about how Gerard and I rode the train to Chantilly. He showed me all the tourist spots, and then we found a little restaurant and ate under a grape trellis by candlelight. We whispered, laughed, and cuddled all the way back to Paris on the train. He told me I was enchanting and that he wanted to wake up every morning to the sunshine fragrance of my hair.

"Then he asked me to go back with him to his apartment that night. I said I couldn't. I had one more day before I flew home. I was expecting him to ask me to change my ticket and stay longer. That's what I was planning to do the minute he asked me. I was ready to give our love all the time it needed to grow.

"When we got off the train at Gare du Nord, I thought we would go to a café for coffee and sit and talk, like we had all the other nights. Instead, he asked again if I would go back to his apartment. I said no, even though I wanted to say yes. He let go of my hand and said, 'I did not expect this of you. Since your answer is no, then my answer is the same.' He kissed me on both cheeks and looked as if he was about to cry. He said, 'I'll never forget you.' Then he turned and walked away."

"He walked away? Just like that? He left you?"

I nodded.

"And you never saw him again?"

I nodded again. "I was so shocked I stood there for a long time. People walked past me like I was a statue. I waited, thinking this couldn't be happening. This was too bizarre. It couldn't be over. Surely he would come back. I told myself he had only gone to buy me a flower or he was playing a joke on me. Finally I went over to a bench and sat down. I stayed at the train station all night, waiting. But he never came back."

There it was. The truth. Out in the open. My humiliating story. "I was such an idiot."

"No you weren't! Lisa, listen to me. You were *not* an idiot! You did nothing wrong. Gerard was the idiot. He didn't treat you honorably. What a cowardly way for him to end the relationship! Please tell me you haven't been thinking all these years that you did something wrong. Lisa, you did nothing wrong."

A wall inside me burst, and a torrent of tears surged forward, determined this time to break down the Bastille of my emotions and release all their fellow captors on the rally toward freedom. I made a mess of the beautiful cloth napkin. I also began to believe for the first time that I wasn't a fool. Amy's simple words of truth were stronger than the lies I had believed for so long. Gerard acted cowardly, not me. Amy was right. There was no shame in falling in love. I had naively floated around for a week in a fairy-tale dream that didn't end happily ever after. That was that. I wasn't a fool. It wasn't my fault. It was just what it was. And it needed to be over inside me.

"Lisa, listen to me. Everything you hoped for in lasting

love is possible. It just wasn't possible with Gerard. Everything you felt was true. Don't disregard the depth of your emotions. You placed your hope on the wrong person, that's all."

"I know. I should have saved my emotions for Joel. Then I could have given him my whole heart without all the scars."

"No." Amy's eyes widened. "That's not what I meant. I was trying to say that the only One who will never leave you and never disappoint you is the One who made you. God. He's the only One who can fill the depths of our hearts. When I realized that my sophomore year of college, it…well, I've told you before. It changed everything. Lisa, there's a big difference between knowing about God and opening yourself up to Him so you can really know Him."

Amy's words didn't settle well with me. Of course I knew that God was supposed to be the most important relationship in my life. Wasn't I the one who took her to a church that taught that? Wasn't I the one who gave her first Bible to her? Why was she telling me that I had to open my heart to God?

I felt as if I had to get out in the cool night air to clear my thoughts. "Amy, I'm ready to go. Are you?"

"That's pretty abrupt." She leaned back, studying my posture. "Are you sure you want to go? We can stay and talk some more if you want."

"No. I'm not trying to be abrupt. I'm just exhausted. Is it okay if we go?"

Amy honored my request, and we left the solace of the special restaurant by thanking our waiter many times over and receiving his assistance in putting on our jackets.

We rode silently in the taxi back to our hotel and went to bed without talking any more about Gerard, love, or telling ourselves the truth. My mind overprocessed everything that night in my dreams. Instead of dreaming of Jerry Lewis directing traffic and Johnny Depp giving Amy a ride around Paris on the back of his Vespa, I dreamed of Joel. I was holding hands with my husband and laughing with him, and he was kissing me on the neck.

I woke up from the sweet dream smiling. All the churned-up feelings that had dominated our dinner were dissipating. In their place I felt hope coming in like morning light through a mist.

I can't say that opening up about Gerard healed me or smoothed away the rough memories. But telling my story had broken down an ancient prison inside me and set my thoughts free. My insides seemed to echo now with the vastness of the open spaces the cleaning out of lies had left.

Amy smiled at me from across the room. She was sitting by the open window reading her Bible. "Morning. How are you feeling?"

"Good." I sat up and smiled at Amy. She was wearing her new cashmere sweater set with her silk scarf around her neck. Obviously, she was ready to go.

"Thank you for listening last night. I probably should

have told you all of that a long time ago."

"Don't start blaming yourself for something new. You're too hard on yourself, Lisa. Whoever said you had to be the first perfect human who ever lived, or that you couldn't make mistakes and figure things out as you went along?"

"My mom," I said without missing a beat.

"Well, your mom isn't here, and she isn't part of the Trinity the last time I checked, so you only have to answer to our heavenly Papa. If His Spirit is telling you that you missed the mark somewhere along the way, fine. Agree with Him. Confess what you did that was out of line. Then thank Him for His generous forgiveness and move on. Don't get stuck. Part of you got stuck here."

"I know." I drew my knees up under the sheet and hugged them. "I knew that yesterday at the Louvre."

"Is that why you cried?"

I nodded.

Amy's smile curved up with a Mona Lisa twist of knowing and tenderness.

"What? What are you smiling about?"

"God is doing something new in you, Lisa. He's onto you. He's pursuing you. I love watching Him do that to people. He's so patient with us. Yet so persistent."

I lowered my voice the way I used to whenever Amy and I told each other secrets. I confided to her the mysterious something I felt at Angelina's when we were having our chocolate party with Jill. I told Amy how I felt as if God was coming to me, brushing past my spirit. I described how I felt like a maverick, doing whatever I wanted while all the molecules between God and me were doing what they were supposed to do and that's why the universe still held in place.

"You're right. We are the mavericks," she said. "All the rest of His creation does what it was designed to do."

"Even gravity," I added with a grin.

"Even gravity," Amy repeated. "But not us. Yet He still comes after us."

We sighed in harmony.

I said I'd take a quick shower so we could get going.

"You should choose where we go for breakfast this morning," Amy called out.

I knew exactly where I wanted to go. A certain sidewalk café on the Champs-Elysées. The one Amy had pointed out a few days earlier. To lift my confidence even more, I donned my pink Parisian top with the black bow at the neckline.

We emerged from the Metro stop a little more than an hour later and were greeted with a fine spring mist coming from puffed-up gray clouds overhead. I stopped at the cart of a sidewalk vendor peddling all the usual souvenirs and purchased a beret. A black one. Classic. Amy followed my example and bought a beret, too. Only hers was pink. And fuzzy. It was kind of funny, and I think she knew that because she tucked it in her purse. I popped my beret on my head and strode toward the café with a certain savoir faire.

"Here," I said, showing Amy my intended destination. "I want to sit here at this table and drink coffee and…"

"And what?" Amy asked after we were seated under a protective awning.

"I don't know exactly. Put to rest an old fantasy, I guess. This is where I decided I was in love with Gerard. I want to sit here and think."

"Okay. Would you mind if I ordered something to eat while you think?"

"Order two of whatever you get, please. And a coffee, of course."

Amy engaged the waiter in a quick request for our breakfast while I took in the view. Yes. This was approximately where we had sat. I drew in a deep breath and concentrated. Car fumes and wet oil on the wide road that separated the two sides of the street. Dark, strong coffee. Slight scent of fresh-baked bread. Heavy, sweet scent of aftershave wafting from the man sitting closest to our table. Cigarette smoke from the man in the suit reading the newspaper. A faint trace of wet dog hair. Floral soap fragrance on the woman moving past our table.

Were these the warm tones and base notes of the elixir that drew young hearts to Paris so they could fall in love? Had I been intoxicated with this scent?

"What does it smell like to you, Amy?"

She sniffed the air slightly and gave me a shrug. "Morning in a big city?"

I looked up and down the boulevard. Morning traffic. Taxis honking. Women with petite umbrellas protecting their hair from the rain. Men in dark business suits looking straight ahead. An ethnic mix of college students standing in a group of four with backpacks on, all studying a map. A small boy in a stroller leaning forward and looking at his little red rain boots. Tulips in bloom in a planter at the shop next to the café.

It was a city. That's all. Not a magical land of love potions in the air. It wasn't Paris that had made me fall in love. It wasn't Gerard. It was me. I fell in love. It just happened to be here. My first brush with heart-searing love happened in Paris. And I happened to fall in love. There was nothing wrong with that.

"Guess what, Amy? I fell in love in Paris."

"So you said last night."

"And so I'll say it again. I fell in love in Paris. There. That was it. No shame in that. It wasn't the fault of Paris or Gerard or me. It was just what it was."

Amy's grin was broad. "Bravo, *mon ami*!" She lifted her coffee cup to salute my brave step in dismantling a tangle of old lies and owning my history without trying to defend or justify it.

"May truth and freedom prevail!" Amy sipped her coffee in my honor.

The man with the newspaper looked over at us with an air of disapproval.

"Why did it take me so long to say that? Why did I cover it up for so long? It's a small truth. A simple reality. What was I thinking?"

"Why did Eve sew fig leaves together and hide behind the bushes?"

"What are you talking about?"

"Adam and Eve. What did they say when God came looking for them, and they were hiding?"

I took a stab at answering a familiar Bible lesson that I should have known by heart. "They said they had sinned and that the snake had tempted them. Then they received their punishment."

"Ooh," Amy said, with that expression on her face that had appeared the night we were eleven and I was so sure I knew where babies came from.

"What? I know the story very well. Adam and Eve were cast out of the garden of Eden because of their disobedience."

"Right. But even after they disobeyed, God came to them. He pursued them. My question to you is, what did Adam and Eve say when they were in the bushes, covered up with the little leaf-outfits they had made for themselves?"

"Is this a fashion question?" I said, trying to take the attention off not knowing what Amy was getting at.

"No, it's not a fashion question. Adam and Eve said

they were afraid so they hid."

"Afraid of what?"

Amy's dark eyes glowed with a warmth that showed up whenever she was very happy and about to get something she had wanted for a long time. "When you know the answer to that, Lisa-girl, you'll have the missing piece you've been looking for. That's when the truth will set you free."

I looked at her over the top of my glasses, trying to make sure I read her expression correctly. "What's with the riddles? What missing piece?"

"No riddle. You asked a good question. You asked why you hid from the truth for so long. If I tell you what I think the answer is, you may not remember it. If you seek the answer, it will come and stay with you."

"That's another riddle."

"No, it's not. You're so close, Lisa. It will all come together for you. Just trust me."

"Oh, I see," I said with a tease in my voice. "This is your chance to finally get back at me for something."

Amy laughed. "No, this is just God doing something new in you, and me trying not to get in the way." Leaning over and sounding confidential she said, "So how am I doing?"

"You're ticking me off," I said with a grin.

"Good." Amy's grin was pure satisfaction. "I wouldn't want today to be any different from any other day."

Seventeen

The morning sky was still a little weepy as we paid for our breakfast and headed for the Metro station and the underground train that would take us to the low hills north of Paris.

Amy and I knew from our abandoned attempt a few days earlier that Montmartre was the hot spot for the Bohemian movement in the 1800s. Starving artists such as Picasso, Renoir, and Toulouse-Lautrec gathered there because rent was low. Vincent van Gogh lived here with his brother for two years. Jill had told us that, when van Gogh came here, he was transformed from a Dutch painter stuck with a pallet of blues and grays to an artist who felt free to go wild with colors and textures.

We also knew about how all manner of debauchery could still be found in the district where the Moulin Rouge dance hall still stood. This was the birthplace of the cancan and the graveyard of a thousand shattered dreams.

I didn't know what to expect when we exited the Metro. What we encountered were more steps than either of us had climbed so far on the trip. We climbed up and up out of the earth and yet once we were out of the Metro station, we still had dozens of steps to climb to reach Sacré Coeur, the "Sacred Heart" white stone church that stood like a beacon at the top of the hill.

"Beautiful," Amy said, panting along with me as we gazed up at the Roman-Byzantine basilica. "Look how beautiful this is!"

"The tour book says that for five euros we can experience a claustrophobic climb up spiral stairs 260 feet to the top." I paused to catch my breath and keep the page from flapping in the tour book. "It says we will be rewarded with a commanding panoramic view of Paris from the dome."

Amy turned around. "I'm looking at a pretty commanding view of Paris from right here."

"Me, too. How are you doing with all the stairs?"

"Much better than I'd be doing if we had to climb ladders to get here. And much, much better than I would have been if we had taken this trip a year ago before the aerobics classes."

We stood in the fine drizzle coming from fast-moving clouds overhead and looked out over Paris. The view changed as the clouds broke open and made room for the sun to spotlight certain districts.

"Let's go find the artists," Amy said.

We followed the map in our tour book and walked several blocks around the large church's back side. Coming into an area that was swarming with tourists, we knew we were in the right place. A restaurant- and shop-lined square was alive with dozens of artists.

Despite the drippy weather, they stood easel to easel under canopies of plastic tarp or wide café umbrellas. Some were young with pleasant expressions and straight postures. Others were closer to the end of their life journeys, heads tilted one direction, clothing and hair expressing their individuality, a look of hazy disconnect in their eyes.

Available artists asked Amy and me in French and then German and then English if we would like our portraits painted. Politely declining each master who stood ready, we strolled around the court, making one big box with our steps. Each artist had a different look or technique. Most had finished works for sale that depicted familiar Parisian sites. Those works were propped up waiting for buyers.

Taking our time and listening to several conversations, we decided this was the place where feisty tourists came to haggle over the price of a painting. Eiffel Towers abounded. Every size, viewpoint, color, and texture of the familiar icon could be purchased at prices that were equally varied.

A small rectangular painting of the Eiffel Tower, no larger than a postcard, caught my eye. It was on a pegboard under a blue tarp along with a dozen other small paintings. I loved the clouds the artist had captured and the definitive surety of the proud Eiffel Tower.

"How much for this one?" I asked the artist.

"Five euros," he said.

Even though it seemed customary to barter, I thought it would be easier to pay the asking price. The truth was, I would have paid twice that. I handed him a five-euro bill and told him the picture was beautiful.

"Merci," he said, his head dipped down.

I wondered if this middle-aged man had dreamed of greatness when he first followed in the footsteps of the artists whose work now hung a few kilometers away in the many Parisian museums. Did he feel he never had accomplished his life goals and now was relegated to this tourist spot, destined to express himself in simple yet masterful bits of art that sold for Metro fare?

My heart went out to him as we continued to admire his other works.

"That one is very nice." Amy nodded at a larger painting of the Eiffel Tower with a background of pink blossoming trees and thin clouds in the deep sky.

I understood what she was feeling. Her love-hate affair with the Eiffel Tower had begun. She was sinking into a quiet place inside herself. I knew all the signs in her as well as I knew them in myself. What was it she had told me that morning? Once I knew why Eve covered herself with fig leaves and hid, I would be free. It seemed Amy needed to solve some tandem riddle to be free as well. Maybe God was pursuing both of us.

Amy went all out and bought four of his eight Eiffel Tower pictures.

"These are really wonderful," I told him. "Very beautiful. You paint clouds that are so peaceful."

"Merci." He nodded his head without smiling.

Amy said something to him in French, and he granted her the smile I'd been trying so hard to extract but had failed to acquire.

"What did you tell him?" I asked as we walked on and took our time viewing a collection of countryside paintings.

"I told him his work showed the depth of his pain."

"And he liked that?"

"Apparently. I was thinking that if I stood outside under constant public scrutiny just for the opportunity to express on canvas what I felt inside, I would want someone to recognize that what I was doing cost me something. I sort of got the idea from something you said."

"Something I said?"

"You said you thought of God as the artist, and we are His maverick subjects. I've been thinking about that. Considering His willingness to not stop expressing Himself out in the open, in front of a world full of critics, I think God's work in us is beautiful. More than that, His work in us expresses the depth of His pain."

"Where do you keep coming up with this stuff?"

She shrugged. "You're the one with all the deep insights, like God being a master artist. I'm just taking what you're saying and adding a few little thoughts."

I wasn't sure what to do with Amy's insights. I knew we were in a corner of Paris that was just made for philosophizing.

Shops full of fun souvenirs also surrounded us. At the moment, the thought of shopping was more appealing than solving my problems, so I urged Amy into the first shop. From there, her shopping instincts took over.

The Rodin Museum was next on our "to see" list. We braved the trek back to the Metro station and found that downhill wasn't nearly as grueling as the uphill had been.

Amy had the Metro stops figured out and led the way to the Rodin Museum. We agreed that the gardens were beautiful, but we were more interested in looking inside. The museum was in the house and studio where this nineteenth-century Michelangelo lived and worked. His statues all expressed a sense of motion. We gazed appreciatively at many of his emotive pieces but quickened our steps to find the statue of *The Thinker*.

"Did you read this?" Amy said. "Twenty-nine authorized copies of this statue make it the most famous statue in the world."

"I think I liked some of the statues at the Louvre more than this one." Glancing at my watch I added, "It's still early. Would you mind if we went back to the Louvre? There's so much we didn't see yesterday."

Amy was all for another round at the Louvre. This time we lasted only a few hours before she said, "What do you think about catching a taxi and going to the Fleur de Lis for afternoon tea?"

"Lovely idea."

"I'm glad you think so because I'm on masterpiece overload. I've seen too much. I'm not appreciating any of it the way I want to."

"A cup of tea would do us good. Have we had anything to eat today?"

"Just the coffee and pastry early this morning at the Champs-Elysées café."

"Then I'm more than ready for afternoon tea."

Off we went to the Fleur de Lis Hotel, where Grandmere had once gone and had to sit up straight and wear gloves.

We didn't have gloves, of course. And we soon realized we were underdressed. But Amy was an expert at sterling posture, so I followed her lead. I adjusted my beret, smoothed back my hair, straightened my shoulders, and walked behind elegant Amy with my chin up.

The hostess showed us to a duo of plush royal blue chairs in a corner near the harp. A small marble-top table between us became the resting place for the china cups of imported tea and the plate of sweets. I left the ordering up to Amy again, with complete confidence that she would have no problem knowing what both of us would enjoy.

My only request was that she order plenty because I was hungry. The server delivered two plates loaded with sweets. We had several kinds of cookies and half a dozen chocolate bonbons as well as a generous slice of some sort of decadent-looking cake. Small cubes of cheese dotted the plates of delicacies along with a large chocolate-dipped strawberry.

"That's odd," Amy said, her shoulders still where they were supposed to be for all women of refinement. "I thought I ordered something different. Something with little sandwiches. This is a whole lot of sugar!"

"Oh, well!" I popped a chocolate into my mouth. "*Bon appétit!*"

"Don't you mean bonbon appétit?" Amy asked.

I could tell we both were feeling pretty uppity.

"Wow!" I said softly as the inside of the bonbon burst open in my mouth. "This is really rich. The filling has a sharp fruity twang to it."

Amy made a little face. "You can have mine then. I don't care for chocolate-covered cherries, if that's what they are."

"I don't know what they are, but the taste is fantastic."

I took small, dainty bites of the scrumptious cake and followed with another bonbon. The harpist plucked an airy tune with her thin fingers. She seemed to know how to gather notes into a melody the way a florist gathers single flowers and turns them into a bouquet.

Amy nibbled on the cookies and sipped her tea. She abstained from her bonbons, so I helped her clear her plate. I had no trouble finding room in my empty stomach for her share and mine of the fruity, creamy chocolates. They were dark chocolate on the outside and inside each had a different flavored center that was syrupy thick yet with a density and tang I'd never tasted before in a chocolate candy.

I poured a second cup of tea and sat up straight, keeping my knees together. I felt as if we were still in third grade and playing a game of grown-up tea party. Glancing around the lounge, none of the other well-dressed diplomats and persons of influence seemed to be playing tea party. They were having tea for real. Two men across from us leaned in toward each other intent on serious discussions that, for all we knew, could have been of strategic importance to world peace.

An African woman entered in a breathtaking native outfit of bright yellow and green cotton fabric. She wore the matching material on her head in a beautiful headdress and walked as if she were a queen. The men in their tailored suits rose when she entered the tea lounge area and greeted her with a kiss on the back of her hand.

"I wonder if this is the sort of afternoon tea Grandmere had here," I whispered to Amy while reaching for yet another bonbon. "Do you suppose people of influence were meeting here seventy years ago when Grandmere came?"

"According to the plaque on the wall when we entered, Benjamin Franklin met King Louis XVI at this hotel to sign some sort of treaty."

Raising my eyebrows to show I was impressed, I tried to lick the corner of my mouth where I'd missed a spot of the fabulous chocolate.

"Benjamin himself!" I said. The buzz I was getting off the candy was making me feel high enough to fly a kite and discover some untapped streak of electrical current. "These chocolates are really something. Are you sure you don't want one?"

"Positive," Amy said. "My stomach is a little upset. We really should have eaten some protein first."

"Is it warm in here?" I asked.

"No, not really. Are you warm?"

I suddenly had to blink to focus my eyes on Amy.

"Are you okay?" Amy looked at me closely. She sniffed twice over the tray of goodies and then picked up the final bonbon.

"I knew you would change your mind," I said. "They are really, really, really good."

Amy took a tiny nip at the chocolate so that the marvelous inner goo oozed out. She took a kitten-sized taste with the tip of the tongue and looked at me with surprise.

"Ooh, Lisa, you should have gone easy on these."

"Too late. Why?"

"I think they're filled with liqueur."

"Are you serious?"

"Didn't they taste that way to you?"

"How would I know?" I didn't feel so well. My stomach wasn't used to receiving such extravagant deposits. "Can we pay for this and get some fresh air?"

"Sure." Amy made a gracious motion for the uniformed server to come over to us. She asked for the check as I rummaged for some euros in my purse.

"Put your money away, Lisa. I'm paying for this one."

"I can contribute," I said. "How much is my half?"

"Let me put it this way. The bonbons alone have a street value of twenty-five euros."

I knew that wasn't good. My stomach wasn't good either. "Amy, thank you," I said, as she signed the Visa bill.

I stood and felt woozy. "Uh-oh."

"You okay?" Amy asked.

"No."

Picking up our pace past the Armani-suited men, I tightly pursed my lips together. My expression must have said it all because, just as we rounded the corner into the lobby by the plaque honoring Benjamin Franklin, Amy assessed the need.

"You're going to lose it, aren't you?"

"Uh-huh," was all I could manage. I was too busy measuring the distance to the front door while scouting out the lobby for possible planters to lean my head over.

Amy pulled off one of her shoes and thrust it over my

mouth and nose. If I hadn't already needed to throw up, I would have then.

Blessedly, I've always been a quiet sick person and not like Amy with her "oohs" and "ohhs." Also blessedly, like the best friend she always has been, Amy stepped in front of me and blocked my performance from the view of any sedate guests.

I urped as quietly as I could in her shoe. One urp was all it took.

"You okay?" Amy whispered.

I nodded, blinking in utter humiliation. I didn't look back into the tea salon to see if my "moment" had caused a hiatus in the world peace negotiations. It seemed better to keep walking and never look back.

"The sign says the restroom is this way." Amy led the way, limping only slightly in her stocking-covered foot.

I held her shoe under my arm the way some diplomats hold a folded copy of the *New York Times*.

"Oh, Amy," I said the moment we were behind the bathroom door. "I threw up in your shoe."

"Yeah, I know. I was there, remember?"

"But how did you know that I was going to throw up?"

"The only other time I'd seen that look on your face was in fourth grade at the Thanksgiving pageant. Remember? Randall Finnley's hat?"

I groaned and rinsed my mouth with water in the sink. Being reminded of the fourth-grade disaster made me feel queasy all over again. Amy and I were part of the chorus group waiting backstage while the star students went onstage dressed as pilgrims and Native Americans. Next to the cardboard turkey they stiffly reenacted the friendly greetings exchanged at the first Thanksgiving. I had turned to Amy backstage a few moments before the performance began, and all I said to her was, "Uh-oh."

Amy took one look at my pale face, grabbed Randall Finnley's pilgrim hat, and held it up to my mouth at the crucial second. It wasn't pretty, but at least it was brief.

Randall Finnley appeared on stage thirty seconds later without his hat. His arms were crossed and he was wearing a puckered scowl. The audience waited for him to deliver his opening line of, "Welcome to the feast." Instead of sticking with the script, Randall reported in his boisterous stage voice, "Lisa Kroeker just urped in my hat!"

I think that was the beginning of the Kroeker jokes with the double meanings.

"Amy, I'm sorry." I wet a paper towel and dabbed the back of my neck.

"Don't worry about it. I never liked these shoes very much." She took off the other closed-heel clog and glee-fully tossed it into the trashcan.

"Amy!"

"Go ahead. Toss the other shoe in there, too. We'll have to go shopping now. Too bad, huh?"

"Shopping?"

"Yes, shopping. I need a new pair of shoes ASAP."

I argued with Amy that we might be able to clean the defiled shoe.

"Lisa, are you kidding? I never could slip my foot into that shoe again. Go ahead, throw it away."

I dropped Amy's shoe into the trash receptacle. "Amy, I don't know what I would have done if you hadn't interceded at the right moment."

"Oh, I have a pretty clear mental picture of what you would have done. Come on, let's ask the concierge where a person in desperate need can buy a pair of shoes in Paris."

A voice with a heavy French accent spoke to us in English from behind one of the closed stalls. "Michelle's on Rue Denon in St. Severin. They have the best selection of shoes. But you will need to hurry. They close at five o'clock."

Amy and I looked at each other with surprise and then in unison said, "Thank you!" We didn't stick around to see who was making the helpful shoe recommendation since we only had half an hour to reach the shop before it closed. Apparently women around the world understand when it comes to shoes.

Trotting out of the world-class hotel in her stocking feet, Amy asked the bellman to hail us a taxi. She did this as naturally as if she were a frequent guest at this fine establishment and always went about the streets of Paris in her stocking feet.

Eighteen

Amy repeated the name of the store and street to the taxi driver. I was glad for her keen memory because I already had forgotten what the mystery woman told us. It took ten minutes to travel across town in the afternoon traffic. Overpaying the driver because Amy didn't want to wait around for change, we dashed into the boutique-style shop and eyed the displayed shoes.

I gazed the way a weary mom stares in her freezer and tries to decide if she's going to thaw a pound of hamburger or a package of chicken wings for dinner. Amy gazed tenderly, like a proud auntie at the window of a hospital maternity ward, eager to figure out which one of the darlings is her new nephew and how soon can she get her hands on his chubby little cheeks.

"These are nice." I picked up a basic brown loafer that

looked like the same style Amy had worn in high school. I always gravitated toward the classic look. That way I could be fairly certain I wasn't going out of style before the clothing wore out.

"Boring. I like these better." She held up a sassy pair of hot pink shoes with a glittery buckle.

I thought she was kidding and said, "And where, exactly, would you wear those?"

"Everywhere! They're adorable. Jeanette would be so proud of me, if I bought these shoes. Or these." She held up a bright yellow shoe with a black bow across the toes. I had to agree. The yellow shoes were darling.

With four potential shoe replacements in her hands, Amy turned to the saleswoman. "May I try these on in a size eight and a half or nine?"

"No," the saleswoman said, glaring at Amy's stocking feet. "We have only European sizes. We do not have eight and a half or nine."

"Okay," Amy said undaunted. She slipped into French and apparently asked the woman to measure her foot to determine her European size. The sales associate was much more agreeable and kept talking with Amy at a fast clip in French.

Task completed, the clerk went off to obtain the selected shoes. Amy looked at me and made a face. "Thirty-seven! How depressing to wear size thirty-seven shoes."

Thirty-seven turned out to be Amy's new best number, as she tried on what seemed like thirty-seven pairs of shoes in her new size thirty-seven. I watched each pair go on and off her feet. I particularly liked the pair of hot pink shoes with black patent leather straps. Extracting them from Amy's reject pile, I nonchalantly slipped one of them on my feet. The ridiculously delectable shoes slid on with Cinderella-fit perfection and made me smile.

"Are they yummy?" Amy asked.

"Amazingly yummy. They're so comfortable."

"And I can see they make you happy. That's Jeanette's criteria, you know. She doesn't buy anything with her own money unless it passes the yummy-happy test. It has to be yummy, and it has to make her happy."

"What about being affordable?" I looked at the price tag and tried to calculate the amount from euros into dollars. If I did the math correctly, the shoes were a steal. "Amy, did I figure out this price correctly?"

Amy checked it and came up with the same price I was calculating. We looked at each other with enthusiasm for our retail experience of the day.

The salesclerk stepped away and returned with a purse that matched my pink shoes.

"That is so stinkin' cute I can hardly stand it!" Amy squealed. "Look how perfectly it matches your pink top."

"I know! This is the cutest purse in the world, isn't it?" I held the perfect-sized pink purse up to my side, as if I were modeling it. The neatly tied black bow looked so snappy. I walked over to the full-length mirror and posed this way and that. I loved it. It was yummy. And best of all, I could afford it. Oh, yeah, this purse was coming home with me.

"Lisa, if you don't buy that purse, I'm going to throw up in your shoulder bag so that you *have* to buy a new purse."

We both burst into laughter, and the salesclerk, who obviously understood English, gave us a peculiar look.

"She threw up in my shoes." Amy turned to the clerk and wiggled her toes. "That's why I came in here in stocking feet." She then repeated her line in French.

The clerk gave Amy and me the kind of look Gerard used to give me. Yes, we were crazy. Americans in Paris. What could we say? After trying to fit in and do everything right, clearly some of our lifetime quirks were ours alone to laugh about.

"You can keep your hands off my shoulder bag," I told Amy. "I'm going to buy the purse."

"And the shoes?" Amy asked.

"But of course," I said, trying to imitate a French accent. I didn't impress Amy, and I definitely didn't impress the salesclerk. "They have to come home together so they can keep each other company."

"I couldn't agree more," Amy said.

I took myself for a happy little walk around the store while Amy tried on more shoes.

"I have to concentrate on these two pairs of shoes and see which ones pass the yummy-happy test." Amy sounded as if she were a rocket scientist conducting an important experiment.

"You could buy both of them," I suggested. "Do they come with matching purses?"

Our saleswoman already had gone to the window to pull out the purse that went with the yellow shoes. She seemed less concerned about our keeping her in the store past closing time since we were making purchases and not just trying on thirty-seven pairs of shoes.

"I think the red ones are my favorite." Amy looked at the dazzling red low-heeled honey of a shoe on her right foot and the classy yellow and black high heel on her left. "But the yellow and black ones make my feet look smaller."

"Are they both yummy?" I asked. "Do the yellow ones make you happy?"

"No. They pinch my toes a little. But the red ones don't."

"There's your answer."

"Jeanette will be proud of us both." Amy slipped on both red shoes and walked around. She stopped in front of the mirror and grinned. Clicking her heels together she said, "There's no place like home. There's no place like home."

"Do you have a matching 'Dorothy' purse?" I asked the salesclerk.

Amy spoke up and explained my question. The sales-clerk brought two purses for our inspection, but neither of them truly matched the shoes. Amy didn't mind. She said the shoes were a world of cuteness all to themselves.

"You know, I did have a bit of an emotional connection going with the black ones."

"I missed the trial run on the black ones," I said. "Let's see them."

Simple, stunning, classy, the black shoes had my vote in an instant. "And just consider all the purse options."

The salesclerk willingly gathered nine purses, and then she stood next to me while we watched Amy give us a fashion show. A black leather purse with a fabulous handle won our vote.

The Dorothy red shoes left the store on Amy's feet, and the pink, happy snappies on my feet kept the parade going.

"You and I are a couple of *très chic* chicks! I'm so glad you were sick on the bonbons."

"You're welcome. Just trying to do my part, you know. But we must remember that you were the one who sacrificed your shoe."

Amy clicked her heels together again. "All in the line of duty. So where should we take our yummy new shoes? The Eiffel Tower?" She slapped her hand over her mouth. "Did I say that aloud?"

"Yes, you did. Does that mean you've been thinking about the 'Awful Eiffel'?"

"Maybe. Maybe I'm thinking that we should find a taxi and just show up there. Then, who knows?"

"Fine. Let's stop a taxi."

"Okay, but don't ask me if I'm going to go to the top."

"Okay."

"I'll decide when we get there."

"Okay."

"And don't try to get me to talk about it."

"Fine."

The taxi delivered us to the street in front of the Eiffel Tower, and we disembarked. Instead of hesitating and looking up, Amy headed across the busy plaza. I kept pace with her in my new shoes while she gave her red hot mamas a brisk workout. She was a woman on a mission, and I was her friend. I would always be Amy's friend, and she would always be mine. Whatever happened in her love-hate relationship with Eiffel, I would still be her friend. I'm sure she knew that. I'm sure she knew that she would always be my friend, as well. Otherwise I don't think Amy's experience would have gone the way it did.

At first she didn't say anything. She seemed to be scoping things out, trying on all the options in her mind, the same way we had just tried on shoes. When Amy paused and looked up, I did the same. When she walked away, I was her shadow. She didn't talk so I didn't talk. At one point I saw a few tears glistening in her eyes. My friend was fighting a fierce battle under this mighty metal structure.

At last she took her place in line at the ticket booth, looking up occasionally. The sun was setting, but hundreds of people continued to snap photos and come and go around us.

The sign above the ticket booth stated the options for those going up. One ticket took viewers to the first level where a snack bar, a few souvenir shops, an exhibit, and a display were open to the public. The restaurant on the first level, Altitude 95, was open only to those with reservations. The person in line in front of us told us that most reservations for that restaurant were made three months in advance.

The more elegant restaurant, located on the second level of the tower, took reservations six months ahead for eager diners who wanted a bird's-eye view of Paris. A series of back and forth stairs connected the first and second levels. From the second level, two elevators ran straight up to the top and back.

Amy stepped out of line. I stayed in line.

She shook her head. I nodded mine. She had gotten so close. I was up to the ticket window, looking over my shoulder at her for direction. She shook her head again. I stepped out of line, and we took a cab back to our hotel where we ordered room service and didn't talk about it.

Later that night, I thought that Amy, the early bird, was sound asleep in the darkness of our room. Well after midnight she turned over in bed and softly said, "Lisa, are you awake?"

"Yes."

"We have issues, you and me."

"Yes, we do."

"Tomorrow is our last day. Our last full day."

"I know."

"Lisa?"

"Yes?"

I thought for sure she was going to make me promise her something. My guess was that she would want me to promise that I'd make her go to the top of the Eiffel Tower before we boarded a plane to go home.

But she didn't ask me to promise anything. All she said was, "We need to pray."

The morning light brought welcome sunshine and that delicious spring freshness that was becoming familiar to us when we opened our bedroom window. Neither of us was hungry. Not even for coffee. We wanted to go to church. The church. Notre Dame. We had decided last night when we prayed together in the stillness, that we wanted—no, needed— to go to Notre Dame.

It wasn't as if God couldn't or wouldn't meet us where we were, whether it was in our hotel room or at a shoe store. But going to a place set apart for centuries as a place of worship was mysteriously sacred. Amy understood this better than I.

We could have walked to Notre Dame. We could have worn hats since we both had purchased berets. We could have carried our Bibles. We also could have taken the Metro, since we had nearly mastered the system. But we took a taxi and sat quietly with our hands folded in our laps all the way there.

I opened the door of the cab and stepped out into the wide courtyard that for centuries had welcomed all pilgrims to the great soaring towers and immense stained glass window that framed the face of Notre Dame. Sunshine broke through the thick clouds and illuminated all the open space.

"I feel small," Amy said as we walked toward the massive open doors of the cathedral.

"I know. Imagine what this place must have felt like to peasants when they came here. It holds ten thousand people."

"I didn't realize it would affect me this way." Amy stopped to look up at the huge rose window.

"Do you want to walk around the outside first? Or go up into the tower to see the gargoyles?"

"Up?" Amy questioned, as if I'd used all my "up" opportunities the day before. "No on the up. Yes on the around."

We circled the mammoth structure, stopping to take pictures of the flying buttresses on the back side.

"Tell me again why these are significant," Amy said. "I don't remember what the tour book said."

"They're for support. It's the only way the Gothic architects could design a structure this large and keep the weight of the roof from pushing the walls outward and destroying the cathedral."

"Support, huh?" Amy studied the beautifully crafted arches. She turned to me. "Lisa, don't take this the wrong way, but you are my flying buttress."

I found no way to take her comment, except the wrong way. "I'm your flying buttress, huh? Well…" No spunky comeback dropped into my mind at that moment.

"You support me," Amy explained. "You're there to keep my roof on and keep my walls from crumbling down. Thanks."

I nodded slowly at the quirky compliment. "In that case, you're my flying buttress, too. What do you say, we keep this to ourselves though."

Amy smiled. The little pixie.

We finished our loop around the cathedral's perimeter and entered with thousands of other visitors who were also making a shuffling journey around the inside.

I felt as if we were two beggar women, two peasants, in need of a place to sit and think. We had come to the right place. The "sanctuary" of Notre Dame. I was so aware of my shrunken size and importance once we were inside the gigantic space. Around us were thousands of pieces of religious art and rows and rows of pews and chairs. Dozens of stands held lit votive candles at private enclaves where even more art was displayed. Over our heads, high above us in this intricately-crafted cavern of stone, rose rounded domed ceilings also decorated. They gracefully, gigantically completed the elegance of this cocoon.

I stood in ant-sized silence, observing details and faces of people from around the world as they made their way through a place that many seemed to consider one of the most exquisite of all the Parisian museums. Yet it wasn't a museum. It was a church. It had been started nearly a thousand years ago with the express purpose of exalting God and providing a place for His people to gather and commune with Him.

Finding an open pew, I lowered myself to the hard wooden bench and sat waiting. Expectant. How would God speak in the overwhelming majestic beauty of this sanctuary?

Nineteen

O*oh!*" Amy's voice beside me brought a sense of the familiar in the openness of Notre Dame. She was nodding toward the immense round window behind me, in the north end of the cathedral. Fragments of sunshine streamed through the stained glass, filling this place of so much empty space with light.

"The Rose Window," she whispered. "It's more amazing on the inside than I imagined. I think that's the window that still has some of its original glass."

I looked up at the window and watched the light come through all those fragments, creating a kaleidoscope of color. Like spokes radiating from a small hub, the images depicted in the huge window were all from the Bible. According to the guide book, the theme of the window was "redemption after the fall."

As I stared at the masterful work of art with a sense of awe, light came through every one of those stories told in pieces of colored glass. Every one was true. Every piece reflected light somewhere in the vast cathedral and had been doing so for more than nine hundred years.

Amy sat beside me, her chin all the way up, staring at the beautifully arched ceiling that was held in place by the flying buttresses.

Beside us rose a huge pillar. A little girl suddenly dashed around the back side of the pillar. A dark-haired man called to the little girl, but she didn't go back to him. Instead she stayed in hiding, covering her face with her hands, as if that would keep him from seeing her.

Eve hid and covered up with fig leaves. Why?

I watched the little girl as she tried to stay in the shadows and not be seen by her father.

I knew that feeling. From the time I had started to help out in the church nursery, I had been trying to stay off of God's radar so He wouldn't come looking for me. I was afraid, and so I hid.

That's it! I was afraid. Eve was afraid. That's what it says in Genesis. Eve was afraid, and so she hid. I get that. I'm afraid. That's why I hide. But what am I afraid of?

I looked into the face of the little girl's father, who came toward the pillar with swift, deliberate steps. His expression was set on her alone and overflowing with love. He didn't want to be separated from his little one.

Calling to her and opening his arms for her, the father waited. From where we sat, I could see what the child behind the pillar could not see. Her papa wanted her back. Now.

The timid child stepped out of hiding with her chin tucked and her eyes lowered. She took the first step. Her father came the rest of the way and scooped her up into his arms.

In that moment, I knew the answer to Amy's riddle. I knew why Eve hid. I knew why I hid. Both Eve and I were afraid of God. Afraid to see His expression of disappointment and displeasure. For Eve it would have been the first time she saw that expression on her Creator's face.

Is that what I've believed all these years? That God is disgusted by me or disappointed in me?

Viewing the earthly father in front of me who was pursuing his wayward daughter, I saw that his intense desire for reconciliation was far greater than his intent to punish.

All these years I had believed a lie. God wasn't mad at me. His anger was momentary, but His lovingkindness toward me was forever. God wanted me.

I always thought I had to prove to God what a good person I was so He wouldn't be angry. That's why I tried to work everything out on my own. I thought I was supposed to be an "A" student and make God proud of me for doing everything as correctly as I could. Yet now I saw the truth. He didn't want my stacks of well-done homework or a report on my commendable behavior. He just wanted me. Now.

I watched as the little girl looked up at her father. He held her close. Speaking to her in gentle tones, he stroked her hair and spoke to her softly, in a language I didn't understand. But the child understood. She looked at her daddy face-to-face and nodded her head, as if in accompaniment to a sincere apology.

He spoke to her again. She spontaneously kissed her papa on the cheek. He smiled, and she rested her head on his shoulder in the curve of his neck. As I watched, he held her close and walked away, carrying her in his arms.

Grace upon grace.

I felt my heart racing the way it had at Angelina's, when I felt as if God was coming close to me. This was it. All my senses were alive.

"I'm here," I whispered, picturing myself as a frightened little girl who had been hiding far too long. In that moment, I stepped out of hiding. The deepest, most timid part of my spirit told God I was sorry. Sorry that I had held back from opening up my heart to Him. Sorry that I had spent so many years hiding.

But my lengthy confession was cut short. All I could think of, and all my senses could feel, was lightness. He was lifting me, drawing me closer and closer. I was in His arms, the very place I had longed to be and never felt I was good enough to go.

All these years I thought You would reject me, too, if I opened up to You like this. But, Father God, You have never left. Never rejected me. This is what You've wanted and waited for all along, isn't it? Not my sterling behavior, but this. This closeness.

The truth began to fill all the hollowed-out places of my soul where the lies had been swept out. Light came in. Light was the missing piece. Lightness in my spirit. This closeness to my heavenly Papa was why I was on this earth. This lasting love would fill the depths of my emotions and set me free.

I didn't realize I was crying. Amy handed me a tissue and gave my hand a squeeze. "What just happened?" she whispered.

I tilted my head and rested it on her shoulder for a moment. I smiled. "I know why Eve hid. I'm not afraid anymore." Swallowing a rising wave of amazement-tears I said, "He wants me. God wants me."

As I looked up at Amy, she grinned. Her dark eyes glowed with the reflected light from the nearby stand of votive candles. I didn't have to explain what had just happened in my heart. She could see right through me. Just like always.

Amy linked her arm in mine, and for a long while we sat where we were, watching all the movement around us. We didn't talk or evaluate or expound. We just sat together, receiving from our Papa.

The rest of the day was like that. All the details of our final afternoon in Paris floated into place and fit together. We investigated a variety of shops in the Latin Quarter, and I felt free. The ghost of "Gerard Past" didn't jump out from around a corner to taunt me. The familiar sense of shame didn't shadow my steps or haunt my choices. I felt free. I was out of the shadows and walking in the light.

We took our time walking along the Left Bank, examining original art for sale as well as an assortment of jewelry, souvenirs, and clothing.

I kept thinking about God. How patient He was. How gracious and how kind. It seemed that I finally knew who I was because I wholeheartedly knew who He was. I was my Beloved's, and He was mine. His banner over me was love.

Amy and I made a loop through the area near the opera house and found an open-air market. I bought three kinds of jams for Joel along with a jar of some sort of special artichokes. Every time I thought about seeing my husband again I felt warm. I was eager to express love to other people now that the wet blanket of shame had been lifted.

By the time our feet were complaining, we had covered considerable ground. I was starving. The decision of where to eat dinner became complicated. While we knew a few options of where to find fabulous food in this city, we were aware there were oh so many more.

"It's your turn to choose," I told Amy. "All I ask is that we go to the hotel first so we can drop off all these bags."

"I'm not sure what I want," Amy said.

"If you say you want frog legs, you might be forced to dine alone this evening."

"No, I'm not interested in frog legs. We've had so much great food." She thought hard. "Would you be bummed if we just went back to the hotel and ordered room service?"

"Of course I wouldn't mind."

"Every time we've ordered from room service it's been great," Amy said. "I love the idea of putting on my jammies and having dinner brought to me. That won't happen once I go home."

Before she suggested eating at the hotel, I had hoped Amy would say she wanted to dine on the Eiffel Tower. While it was too late to check on last-minute reservations at one of the main restaurants, we always could have eaten at one of the snack bars.

Apparently Amy would have to come to terms with the Eiffel Tower on her own. I wasn't going to push her or fight with her about it. She was up against fear the same way I had been for so long. If I was afraid of God's disapproval, what was Amy afraid of? Gravity?

We went back to our room. I packed while Amy took a relaxing soak in the bathtub. Dinner was delivered, and we dined in our pj's on salad, bread, chicken Marseilles, and crème brûlée for dessert. Instead of eating on our beds, we pulled the chair from the desk over to the corner chair by the window and balanced the plates on our laps, as if we were at some fancy buffet party.

The view from our hotel room window was dramatic. The City of Lights gave us her best performance. The skies were clear. The spring night was gorgeous. Despite the sound of car horns and the smell of traffic that rose through our open window, a slight scent of fragrant blossoms and rain-softened earth greeted us as well.

Amy chatted about her children and what all of them had said when she called home earlier. "I can't wait to give everyone the gifts I bought. The only problem is, how am I going to fit everything in my suitcases? I brought way too much with me. But you already knew that."

"At least you were prepared," I said.

"Overprepared is more like it. I wonder if I could leave anything here. Or maybe I could mail some of my lighter T-shirts and things home."

"Or," I suggested, "you can go to the souvenir shop on the corner and do what I'm probably going to do tomorrow. I'm going to buy a lightweight carry-on bag for everything that won't fit in my luggage."

"Great idea."

Leaning back and studying Amy's slumping posture, I asked, "Are you okay?"

"No. Yes. No. I don't know. I will be. I'm not ready to leave, but I'm ready to go home."

"Is there anything else you want to do? Anything you want to see? Anything…"

"I know what you're getting at, Lisa, and my answer is still no."

"Okay." I went over to my bed and stretched out under the covers. "I have a question for you, though."

"What?" Amy looked at me skeptically. I knew that expression.

"Why do you think Eve hid?"

"Lisa…"

"No, I'm just asking. You asked me, and now I'm asking you. Why do you think Eve hid?"

"She was afraid." Amy appeared to dislike the taste of her words.

"Okay. That's what I thought, too. Good night."

"You're going to sleep now?"

"Yes. You can leave the light on while you pack. It won't bother me. I'm going to sleep soundly tonight." I turned off the light by my bed. With my eyes closed, I talked with my heavenly Papa, closely and honestly. One of the things I talked to Him about was Amy.

I fell into a peaceful sleep, which was a surprise, since I'd been a night owl since we had arrived. If I was having dreams, crazy or calm, I didn't remember any of them. What woke me was the sound of Amy's sniffling. I rolled over and saw her standing by the window in her pajamas, wrapped up in the hotel's plush robe. Her gaze was fixed on the lit-up Eiffel Tower that dominated the horizon.

I don't know how I knew what to do next, but I knew. Maybe my years of being Amy's friend made my steps certain. Maybe my heavenly Papa nudged me. Maybe it was both.

Rising quietly, I went over, put my arm around Amy, and gave her a hug. Then I turned on the light, went to her packed suitcase, and lifted out several of her stacked clothes. She didn't ask what I was doing, nor did she protest. I unfolded her beautiful, Grace Kelly golden dress and laid it out on her bed. Then I went looking for her new black shoes and matching purse. I found her fuzzy pink beret and stuffed it in my purse.

Going to my suitcase, I pulled out my skirt, my new pink shoes, and the silver box with my new white blouse. I made sure my beret was in my purse as well.

We dressed in silence. I looked over at Amy. She smiled at me.

"Come on," I said after she had on everything but some cheerful lipstick. "You can keep an icon waiting only so long."

Without a peep Amy followed me out of the hotel room. Her dress swished when she walked. Her new shoes tip-tapped on the tile floor in the lobby. She smelled rich, and she walked as if she were royalty, with her shoulders back and her chin forward.

We silently rode in the taxi.

Stepping out of the car and into the glow of the brightly lit Eiffel Tower, I walked to the short line of people buying tickets to go up into the tower. We had an hour before the elevators closed at midnight. Amy stepped in line with me. I opened my happy new purse, pulled out my last fifty-euro bill, and paid for two tickets to the top. We stood in line for the first of three elevator rides. The elevator door opened, we stepped in, and stood beside each other in our dazzlingly yummy new shoes.

A variety of other late-night Eiffel Tower fans joined us. We were by far the best dressed of the bunch. That meant we received a few stares. Especially Amy. She didn't mind. The door opened, and we walked out onto the first level into a space that felt solid and stable. Amy was doing just fine.

Taking our time to proceed to the next elevator that would transport us up to the next level, Amy nudged closer to me. "Lisa, am I on the Eiffel Tower?"

"Yes."

"That's what I thought."

"How does it feel?"

"It's okay. I'm not afraid."

I smiled the way she had smiled at me earlier that day in Notre Dame. I knew what she was feeling. Light. Free.

She looked to the right and then a little bit to the left. "I'm on the Eiffel Tower, Lisa. I'm standing on the first level of the Eiffel Tower, and I'm not freaking out. Look, that's

Paris down there. I can do this. Hey, that's a new verse for the dieter's cards with Shirleene! 'I cancan do all things through Christ who strengthens me.'"

"I take it that's the French version."

"Of course."

"Next elevator is this way," I said with a wide, sweeping gesture.

Amy shocked me when she said, "Let's take the stairs."

"Really?"

She nodded. "Really."

We followed the sign to the stairs and began a journey upward that had me speechless. The metal stairs with the open metal girders on the sides let all the night air come rushing in so that our legs grew cold quickly. We took a set of eight stairs up, then a short landing, then a turn and eight more stairs. We kept climbing, both holding on to the railing. The optical illusion was freaky. Dots of light illuminated the sides of the airy metal structure and more dots of light appeared beneath our feet where the streets of Paris stretched out below. The higher we went, the queasier I felt. Why wasn't Amy having a problem with this?

"You okay?" I asked as we caught our breath on one of the short landings.

Amy's face was radiant in the glow of the lights coming from all directions. "Yes. I'm more than okay. I'm climbing the Eiffel Tower!"

"Yeah, you are." I personally would have done much better with an elevator ride that popped me out at the final destination. But this was typical of Amy. When she went for something, it was all the way. Step by step she was conquering her fear of heights, and I was trying hard not to take on the phobia she was defying.

We reached the second level. Amy was unstoppable now. With every step, her elegant gold dress made a ruffled swish. Her sassy shoes clicked across the metal platform as if they owned the place.

"More?" she asked me, as if I was the one who needed coaxing.

"Elevator is over there," I said, catching my breath and nodding at the line of others waiting for what suddenly felt to me like a rocket ship to the moon.

The line moved steadily. We looked around, standing close together but not saying anything. The elevator wobbled slightly as we packed inside. Holding on to one of the side rails, I smiled at Amy as she swallowed and smiled back. The doors opened, and we stepped out onto a narrow platform that was surrounded by safety bars and mesh netting. My heart pounded as we took a step closer to the guardrails and grasped them in unison. Aside from being in an airplane, I had never been this high before. All the world seemed to spread out before us in a dazzling display of twinkling lights.

Amy held the guard bar with one hand and grasped

my arm with the other. We both caught our breath, looked at each other, and laughed.

"You did it, Amy!"

She laughed the laugh of freedom.

"To commemorate this moment, I have a little something." I pulled her pink beret from my purse. "This is an essential component in our rite of Eiffeling."

"Eiffeling?"

"Just lower your head a minute." Clearing my throat and not caring what the other tourists thought, I proceeded. "Amelie Jeanette, for being a faithful friend, a heroine of the French Republic revered by honest taxi drivers and policemen on Vespas, a defender of the nauseous, and an overcomer of childhood fears, on you I bestow the first ever *Oui Oui Mon Ami* Award for bravery and loyalty beyond the call of duty!" With that, I placed the fuzzy pink beret on the top of her head, tilting it just so.

"I feel like a poodle," Amy said. "But on behalf of Sisterchicks everywhere, I accept this esteemed award."

She reached for my beret peeking out of my purse. "Your turn. Bow, Lisa Marie—and I do mean *Marie*. Ahem. I now present you with the one-of-a-kind Flying Buttress Award for outstanding accomplishments in keeping a lifetime of promises to your dearest friend, renouncing fear with clear-hearted honesty, and assisting finicky eaters of random Parisian bistros by cleaning their plates!"

My beret was plopped in place and tilted a little to the

right. The moment was sealed with a picture that I took of both of us by holding my camera at arm's length and snapping.

Laughing and linking our arms, Amy and I turned to face the vast expanse that sprawled far, far below us. Paris was tucked under a blanket of light. And we were standing above her, looking down on her patchwork of twinkling diamonds from the top of the Eiffel Tower.

We both had waited a lifetime for this trip. This moment.

In unison, without prompting, Amy and I put our shoulders back, tipped our chins high, and with one mighty breath we held on to our berets and shouted, "Ooh la la!"

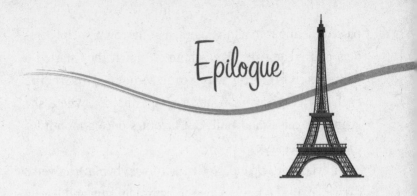

Epilogue

When I returned home, I unfurled all the details for my husband. I told Joel without a hint of shame that I had fallen in love in Paris twice. The first time was with Gerard. The second time I fell in love with God. I told Joel it wasn't as if I didn't already know God or trust Christ or believe that I was saved. I told him I'd come out of hiding, and that fear and shame no longer covered me. I was covered with grace.

Joel cried. I'd only seen him cry a few times.

Over the next few years, our marriage flourished as it never had before. My growing love for my heavenly Papa fueled me with an unending supply of love for Joel.

Amy lost another ten pounds and has stayed at that comfortable weight for the past two years. She and Shirleene made up packets of their special verses. Instead of Diet Verses Shirleene renamed them Soul Snacks and passed them out to all the women at the Lighten Up! aerobics class. The gang liked them so much they started a verse exchange the way some women do a recipe exchange. Each woman has a recipe file box where she keeps her verses and pulls out favorites once a month for the verse exchange.

I even participate. Not in aerobics, but in the verse exchange. I keep my box by the bathroom sink and have a frame by the mirror so I can change the verses once I memorize each one. Last week I told Amy I'd memorized thirty-seven of the Soul Snack verses. She said she had memorized fifty-two. I told her she was an overachiever. She said it took one to know one. I spent a whole day trying to find a verse that said, "Don't get sassy with me, young lady," so I could use that one for my next Soul Snack exchange. It turns out that isn't actually a verse, like my mother always said it was.

The other fun change in Amy since our trip to Paris has been her biannual presentations to the French classes at the high school. I went with her the first time she gave her presentation of Paris, complete with pictures of the two of us. She started off with the account of our luggage riding off with the driver who stole the taxi and ended, not with the story of how she victoriously scaled the Eiffel Tower, but rather with the story of my goof at the local bistro and the sign that said, "Please place your dirty dishes here." Amy gave the students the punch line in French. The quick ones, who did the translation in their heads, whispered the meaning to the others, and all eyes were soon on me as chuckles floated around the room. Yeah, I don't go with her anymore when she does her presentations.

But I do go shopping with her. More often than we used to. Amy and I have both developed a funny little delight in yummy shoes that make us happy. No pair will ever take the place of my Paris Pinkies, as Amy now calls them. But we do have fun looking for a pair that comes close. And the pink purse is still in use. Jeanette borrowed it once and said she was proud of me for being so fashionable.

Probably the biggest change of all since our trip to Paris has been my involvement at church. I no longer help with the nursery. I came out of hiding, so to speak, and began to teach a class on Sunday for the teenage girls. They love the attention and having a group just for them so they can openly ask all their questions. A bunch of them come by the house every chance they get. I love being involved in their lives. I love speaking truth to them. I love watching some of them open up and step away from wrong thinking. The truth starts to shine like a light in their eyes when they see how tenaciously God has been pursuing them. Some of them have horrible situations at home. I love telling them how their heavenly Papa will never leave them and never betray them.

Last Friday eight of the girls came over for a pajama party. I pulled out my beret and told them how this was the same beret I wore in our picture from the top of the Eiffel Tower. They looked at me as if I were the coolest middle-aged woman on the planet. Either that or the craziest. All of them want me to take them to Paris. Who knows? Maybe Amy and I will organize another adventure one of these days.

When I went into the kitchen to make popcorn, Amy's younger daughter, seventeen-year-old Lizzie, followed me. "Aunt Lisa, what do you do if you really, really like a guy, but he doesn't like you back the same way?"

My heart felt free. I looked her in the eye. "You have yourself a good cry, and then you go on. If you're quicker than I was, and I know you are, you'll transfer all those emotions to the only One who will never leave you. Love God first and the most. Keep your heart full of His light, and you'll mend. You really will."

Tears filled her eyes. "That's what my mom says. But it hurts so much. She doesn't understand that part. She said you would understand."

I took her in my arms and drew her close. With a depth of love and honesty I'd not known or understood until my second trip to Paris, I gave my best friend's daughter the gift her own mother wasn't able to give. I cried a few tears of sympathy and whispered into her silky hair, "I know, Lizzie. I really do. But if you keep your heart open to God and to others, you'll be okay. The hurt eventually will go away."

She pulled back. "Do you promise?"

"Yes, I promise."

A thin trace of hope formed a Mona Lisa smile on her adolescent lips. She believed me because I was telling the truth.

Maybe one day I would tell her my story. But not that night. That night she was going to open up and tell me her story. I knew that when she did, I would be given the privilege of speaking truth over Lizzie the same way her mother had spoken truth over me in the City of Lights. That truth would continue to set free. Free to mend and free to love again.

I gave Lizzie my full attention and knew that she and her sister, Jeanette, would be the fourth generation of DuPree women whom I adored.

I told her I have a theory that every promise is heard in the celestial courts. Every promise has the potential of becoming eternal. It is very possible that God really does listen when young girls make "forever friends" promises under the pink ruffles of a canopy bed.

As a matter of fact, I wouldn't be surprised if every time one of those promises is fulfilled, a couple of angels stand side by side looking down on all of us twinkling bits of humanity spread out like diamonds far, far below them. I can just imagine how they might link their arms, tip their wings back, lift their chins, and proclaim at the top of their heavenly voices, "Ooh la la!"

Discussion Guide

1. As little girls, Amy and Lisa thought that walking down the Champs-Elysées and visiting Grandmere's homeland would make them classy and refined. What symbolized "having arrived" to you when you were young? Did you ever do it, and how did it compare to your expectations?

2. Lisa reflects that every promise can be heard in the celestial courts, which gives every promise the potential of having eternal significance. What earthly promises have had eternal significance in your life? Why do you think promises matter to God?

3. Amy works very hard to lose weight before the trip to Paris. Have you struggled with weight gain? How has it affected your willingness to pursue your dreams? How have you been helped by supportive friends like Lisa and Shirleene?

4. Describing their childhoods, Lisa says that her life "provided Amy with roots in the richness of this good earth," while Amy offered her "butterfly wings to soar above it all." How have your friends offered you things you needed? How have you been able to enrich their lives in return?

5. When Amy prays that their luggage would be returned, Lisa wants to tell her not to bother God with this. Do you ever feel like your concerns are too petty for God to care about?

6. By going to Paris and visiting the du Bois family and the shops on Rue Cler, Amy catches a new glimpse of her grandmere's life. Have you ever visited a faraway place special to past generations in your family? What gifts did that experience bring to your life?

7. Lisa comes to realize that she has been afraid of God. In Notre Dame, she sees a little girl hiding from her father, and the father's loving, joyous determination to pursue his daughter helps Lisa understand this dynamic between her and God. Have you ever had an earthly scene help you understand God better? What was it, and what did you learn from it?

8. Lisa says that the gift of a true friend is seeing who you are inside and who you can become. Who among your friends have seen you this way? How has that affected you?

9. Lisa talks about waiting to approach God until she's sure He'd be proud of her. Are there reasons you wait to approach God? What are they?

10. Lisa's mother planted eggplants and parsley in the "garden of life," while the DuPree women planted daffodils and forget-me-nots. What are you planting in the garden of life? And how is it affecting your children?

11. Amy's grandmere says, "Hope is the most versatile and sparkling of all accessories and can be worn by any woman, regardless of her age." How do you accessorize with hope in your own life?

12. Lisa comments later that Amy wraps her "in the accessory that is even more versatile and lovely than hope"—acceptance. Who have you wrapped in acceptance lately? Is there anyone in your life who needs to be wrapped up and embraced in this way?

13. God is described in the book as the Artist, and we as people as His maverick subjects, the ones who resist Him. How have you been resisting His creative touch in your life? What does He want to free you from? What might that look like in your life?

14. Lisa gave Amy her first Bible. Later in life, it's Amy who gives the Bible back to Lisa again and again as the truths of God's Word come springing out in her life. Do you have friends who you've gone back and forth with in this way? How so?

15. Lisa comes to realize that in the years since Gerard rejected her, she has guarded her heart so tightly that she hasn't given it freely to God or to those she loves and trusts. Have you guarded yourself in this way? Has God freed you from a situation like this? How did your life change as a result?

16. In Paris, both Amy and Lisa face their fears and some old wounds: Amy's fear of heights and Lisa's fear of God and her grief over Gerard's rejection. Are there fears and old wounds in your life that you are ready to face?

17. Lisa's longtime view that God requires perfection from us was shaped by her mother's judgment of her. Have you known Christians with a judgmental attitude? How did they affect you? How do you think their attitude affects their own lives?

18. When Amy and Lisa were teenagers, Amy's mother encouraged her not to do anything that might alienate Lisa from her mother. But when they reconnect years later, Lisa tells Amy that she's always felt alienated from her mom and still does. Have you gone through seasons of alienation from your mother? What kind of season is your relationship in right now?

19. Amy and Lisa's trip to Paris is the fulfillment of a childhood promise. Have you had childhood promises fulfilled in unexpected ways? What were they?

More SISTERCHICK® Adventures by
ROBIN JONES GUNN

SISTERCHICK n.: a friend who shares the deepest wonders of your heart, loves you like a sister, and provides a reality check when you're being a brat.

SISTERCHICKS ON THE LOOSE!

Zany antics abound when best friends Sharon and Penny take off on a midlife adventure to Finland, returning home with a new view of God and a new zest for life.

SISTERCHICKS DO THE HULA!

It'll take more than an unexpected stowaway to keep two middle-aged sisterchicks from reliving their college years with a little Waikiki wackiness—and learning to hula for the first time.

SISTERCHICKS IN SOMBREROS!

Two Canadian sisters embark on a journey to claim their inheritance—beachfront property in Mexico—not expecting so many bizarre, wacky problems! But they're nothing a little coconut cake can't cure...

SISTERCHICKS DOWN UNDER!

Kathleen meets Jill at the Chocolate Fish café in New Zealand and they instantly forge a friendship. Now Robin Jones Gunn reveals their crazy adventures in classic Sisterchick style!

www.sisterchicks.com